D0891670

The Hippodrome

Other books by Cyrus Colter:

The Beach Umbrella (stories)

The Rivers of Eros (a novel)

HOUSTON PUBLIC LIBRARY

The Hippodrome

a novel

Cyrus Colter

THE **SWALLOW PRESS** INC.

CHICAGO

HOUSTON PUBLIC LIBRARY

R0151680277
HUM

Copyright © 1973 by Cyrus Colter
All rights reserved
Printed in the United States of America

First Edition
First Printing

Published by
The Swallow Press Incorporated
1139 South Wabash Avenue
Chicago, Illinois 60605

This book is printed on 100% recycled paper

ISBN 0-8040-0625-3
LIBRARY OF CONGRESS CATALOG CARD NUMBER 72-96164

To

MICHAEL ANANIA
Artist-Editor, Friend

Hippodrome—historically an open-air racecourse, with tiered seats, for horse or chariot races. The term is also used colloquially to designate an indoor or outdoor circus and an arena for equestrian performances. . . . The most famous were the Circus Maximus in Rome and the Hippodrome in Constantinople. The latter was 129 yards wide and between 400 and 460 yards long. It accommodated from 60,000 to 100,000 spectators in 30 to 40 tiers of marble seats. . . . The full program normally included chariot races, wrestling, boxing, running, jumping, and gladiatorial combats.

—ENCYCLOPEDIA AMERICANA

The police siren seemed to hoot directly above him and with a wild gasp of exertion he snatched the manhole cover far enough off to admit his body. He swung his legs over the opening and lowered himself into the watery darkness.

—RICHARD WRIGHT, *The Man Who Lived Underground*

A real panic took hold of me. I didn't know where I was going. I ran along the docks, turned into the deserted streets in the Beauvoisis district. The houses watched my flight with their mournful eyes. I repeated with anguish: Where shall I go? . . . where shall I go?

—JEAN-PAUL SARTRE, *La Nausée*

It would pain me to have to say that men are my brothers. The word sickens me because it attaches me to men by an umbilical cord; the word binds us through the mother, then thrusts me back into the womb.

—JEAN GENET, *Miracle of the Rose*

Chapter 1

H E was in flight to nowhere. His very brain tissue seemed abraded, his ankles swollen and putrescent. It was as if he had been fleeing a killer leopard in a nightmare; he was all but wringing with the perspiration of madness and his hot feet were stinging. His heart lurched weakly, thudding and fluttering against his ribs as if victim of a thrombus, and his palms oozed cold sweat. Yet he had really come from the hotel in a taxicab, alighted willynilly, and now, quaking and exhausted, sat atop a fireplug waiting for a bus to come along. He gazed up past the drab apartment buildings to the east. They were ash-colored and archaic in a dawn that somehow seemed to have come too early for the sun, whose rightful place was still strewn with ragged clouds lying in crimson streaks across the sky. The snowing had almost stopped now. Only a few lazy flakes came down to settle onto the wet sidewalk and the eerie scene of grey.

He clutched the package that was under his arm—a solid spherical item wrapped in thick brown paper—and spat. Sitting there, more saliva bubbling on his whispering lips, he placed the package down on his knees and took the half-pint whiskey bottle out of his overcoat pocket. After

1

holding the whiskey for a moment, still whispering, he uncapped it and drank off the inch of fire that remained, then, shuddering, started to toss the empty bottle over the curb, but, further arousing himself, instead returned it to his pocket. Though observing little or nothing, he stared from under the brim of his hat up toward the intersection, where the traffic light beyond the drug store blinked from amber to green. But there was not a pedestrian or a moving car in sight. Now his gaze swept the buildings directly across the street: a small grocery displayed its food stuffs through lighted, barred windows; and next to it the tailor-shop looked seedy; and adjoining, now darkened, was a combination barbecue joint and pool hall. Beyond that a laundromat.

He gazed at all these objects yet saw nothing. His blunted mind was back inside the hotel room where both lustful bodies, sprawled crude and naked—the man's eyes open as in life—lay athwart each other on the bloody bed where he had left them.

Even now his knife hand trembled. He sat curiously staring at it for a moment, the right, then thrust it in his overcoat pocket for more whiskey, and remembered there was none. He lit a cigarette then and, hungrily drawing on it once, absently held it in the scissors of two fingers until over an inch of ash had dropped off at the curb. At last he felt the early March chill of the streets penetrating his ribs and shoulder blades, and shivered; the cold, crude fire-plug he sat on had furrowed his buttocks. Soon, as he peered down the street for the bus, he became convinced that his sanity was extinct, and lifting his face to the sky, shut his eyes and softly ground his teeth when a big snow-flake landed on his eyelid and still another on his nose. Vainly swiping, he muttered something about a God with-out mercy, then a phrase about pity, and rich men, and about foul, betraying bitches, and finally some whispering, broken idiom about the very earth's destruction. Then he tried to restrain, suppress, subdue himself as he wondered whenever the bus did come, where he would go. It had been only minutes before that a police prowl car had approached him. But he had crushed his package closer to his ribs and stood perfectly still. As the car had come alongside him, one of the two policemen inside was finish-ing a sleepy hippopotamus yawn and merely glanced in his direction as the car cruised on past him and through the green light.

At last the bus was coming! He quickly fumbled some change out of his pocket and stood waiting. But when the bus drew opposite him, his legs went weak, ropy, and he stumbled getting on. And after dropping the coins in the fare box, he pitched into the first seat he came to, imme-diately behind the driver. He stared vacantly at the passing pawnshops, small haberdasheries, the dinky hardware stores, the beauty parlors, fried chicken shacks, the scarred, abandoned buildings, hardly recalling his own identity—he only knew he was the man in flight. There were four other passengers on the bus—his fellow blacks —who, on their way to work, were casual and detached as they gazed straight ahead and smoked their after-breakfast cigarettes. He saw very few people elsewhere on these streets and side streets of the fetid ghetto.

When the bus passed a restaurant that had not yet opened for the day, he at last remembered his hunger. He had not eaten since noon of the day before—had been too obsessed with the slow, cunning, implacable pursuit of them. A few minutes later the bus stopped to take on three more passengers and as it pulled away he glimpsed in the next block ahead the big bright-blinking sign of "Kitty's Kafeteria." He stood up at once and pulled the signal cord, and then, still hugging the package to him, stumbled back to the rear door and got off. As he crossed the street he shuffled noticeably, dipping a shoulder and dragging one leg, and his overcoat was thrown open wildly despite the damp cold.

He entered the cafeteria. It was a big, gloomy, high-ceilinged place, ancient and dingy, with its crude mural behind the steam table so murky from the kitchen's smoke that its detail could hardly be made out. The long night had left but one customer, a seated drunk, who would stare into space, laugh to himself, then follow each laugh with a huge, gleeful shrug. The man in flight to nowhere, in a daze, looked around for a clean table, for but few of the night's dirty dishes had been cleared away. Finally sighting one across against the far wall, he went over, put his package down on the chair, and took off his overcoat and threw it on top of the package. Then he shambled up to the steam table.

The only employee left on duty was a shriveled, sleepy, little black man, who stood behind the victuals wearing a white coat and chef's tall bonnet. The man in flight got silverware and took a tray off the stack, then, looking over at the assortment of greasy foods, finally indicated chicken and noodles. When he had paid he carried the tray of food back to his table. Across the room from him now the drunk was asleep, his head on his arm on the table. The man sat down and soon began to eat, chewing very slowly so that his stomach would not reject the food. Yet somehow between mouthfuls his lips still moved in desperate whispers and his head lolled crazily from side to side. The place was morgue-quiet. The little chef had already disappeared into the kitchen—perhaps for another snooze. And up front beyond the big plate glass window the snow was still gently falling against the queasy light of the street lamp in the dawn. He was hungry, yet seemed unable to savor the food, and soon stopped eating, although his plate was still half full. At last he began to eat again, with a slow, bovine mastication, as his dead eyes hovered in the general direction of the water cooler yet saw nothing. It was twenty minutes before his plate was finally empty. After sitting for a few moments more, he got up still as if in a dream, hitched up his trousers, and, limping again, started back up to the steam table for more coffee.

It was then that the two women entered the cafeteria. The girl was in front. Not over twenty-five, she was attractive enough—with smooth brown skin and a passable figure. But the woman behind her, at least thirty-five or six, was huge, muscular, and black—brutal-looking. Both wore naturals, heavy eyebrow make-up, and were tawdrily dressed. They soon got silverware and trays.

The sleepy little chef came out again now and stood waiting behind the steam table, as they studied the food and consulted each other. Meantime the man in flight, empty coffee cup in hand, waited listlessly in line behind them, occasionally mumbling to himself, shifting his puny weight about, and trembling. At last the women chose hash and fried potatoes, and after paying, stood looking around for a clear table. His was the least littered, and unoccupied; they headed over to it, and when he returned, they had already unloaded their trays and were taking off their coats. They looked curiously at him as he sat down with his coffee across from them, for it was only then that they saw his overcoat on the chair beside him.

"S'all right for us to set here, ain't it," the big black woman, in a heavy masculine voice, stated rather than asked.

He only glanced at her, and vaguely nodded.

But soon the women were oblivious of him as they ate and talked; the big woman chided the younger one. "Darlene, you gotta stop burnin' the candle at both ends. You wouldn't be comin' home yet if you wasn't with me. You gotta stop throwin' your time away for nothin'. And yourself too. You never have learned the value of money. Remember, you ain't nothin' without some money. If a bastard can't bring ten or fifteen dollars with him when he comes ringin' my doorbell, he ain't gonna get in."

"Oh hell, Bea." Darlene gave a cynical laugh.

"I'm tellin' you, you can't keep it up," big Bea said. "You never saw me out this late before with no money involved, did you? . . . with my doctor warnin' me all the time about my high blood pressure and to get my rest and keep takin' them pills he's got me on. Sure, I'm out sometimes, but it's strictly business. Then this same damn doctor comes callin' me up tellin' me to go set up all night long last night with Aunt Maudie—can you beat that!—or else. I'da been home in bed way before midnight. That's why I wanted you to come along, so I'd have somebody to talk to and keep me awake. You just gotta get your rest, Darlene, so on our work nights you'll be fresh and rarin' to go—we got our hands full, as it is, operatin' at the house three nights a week, without you playin' around on the side." They talked for fifteen minutes, and when they finished eating they sat and smoked, and slender Darlene toyed with her fancy, plastic cigarette case.

But soon Bea was watching the man in flight. His hat still on, he was fidgeting in his chair and muttering to himself again, and whenever he tried to sip the coffee, he was nearly thwarted by a shaking hand—there was coffee in the saucer and a trickle on his chin. At last he appeared vaguely to notice the women, and seemed riled at the lewdness of their conversation, curling his lip once in hostility. But then almost immediately he lapsed into his former agitation. Soon too he was patting his pockets for cigarettes, then seemed to remember they were in his overcoat on the chair beside him. When he reached for the coat, he took it by the bottom instead of the top, and the empty half-pint whiskey bottle fell out on the floor.

The women stopped talking and looked at him. The bottle had not broken but had skittered across under their feet. Finally big Bea bent down and felt around until she found it. When she saw that it was empty, she grinned at him vindictively—"Gonna take it back and get the deposit on it, eh?"

Veins of rage stood out in his forehead as he snatched the bottle from her and discarded it on the next table. But when he turned back around to them, their faces were caught in a curiously strange expression—they were staring at his right hand. When he looked, he saw what in his delirium he had not noticed before—that his shirt cuff, protruding two inches, was soaked with blood.

The women gaped now.

Breathing hard, he leered, then glared at them.

At last Bea sat back in her chair. "Well, it sure ain't your blood," she said to him. "You ain't got a scratch."

"Shut up, Bea!" Darlene said fearfully. "It's none of our business."

He sat there—his body thin, wasted. He watched them with hollow red eyes. His face had a two day growth of stubble which he scratched and chafed now with fingers scorched by cigarettes. "... What's the matter? ... huh?" he said almost incoherently. "... Are you afraid of blood?"

Bea hesitated. "No ... not exactly," she said. "I'm 'fraid of you, though."

He wrinkled his nose and spoke with slow malevolence. "That shows, then, you're a *smart* whore."

Darlene gasped again.

But Bea eyed him coolly. "No, I'm just smart—period. That's why I *ain't* a whore."

Already he seemed not to hear her and turned and

glared down at his coat and package as if deciding to leave. But suddenly with a dazed stare he shot his hand forward on the table so that they could see the cuff again. "That's not all the blood!" he said, and quickly stood up and showed them the dark stains on his clothing. ". . . Even this is nothing—nothing! You have not *seen* any blood yet!"

Bea studied him. "I wonder if the police ain't lookin' for *you,* Mister," she said, and glanced casually, but warily, around for her coat.

Standing there, he suddenly began trembling again. His eyes, bloodshot, dilated, stared at them with a wildness they had never seen before. They sat transfixed. Then he almost choked in trying to speak, as his whole body shivered. ". . . wait . . . wait! . . ." he whispered. He reached and flung his overcoat off the chair. They saw the package. Clumsily, fumblingly, he began unwrapping it, and soon took out a woman's severed head.

Darlene gave a stifled scream.

Bea stood up—"*Jesus Christ!*"

He set the head on the table, but it toppled over on its side. It was a yellow, flat-nosed, youngish woman. The eyes were closed as in repose, and, except for a few light smears, the face was free of blood. He stood viewing it anew with an oddly curious interest, then let out the deep, heavy breath of a sigh. "She'll never climb in bed with another white man, will she?" he said—almost reflectively. "And he'll never climb in bed again with anybody—not even his *own* wife." He shivered again and gave them the vacant stare.

Finally Bea recovered her speech. "Come on, Darlene! —let's get outa here!" She grabbed her coat off the chair. He now methodically rewrapped the head in the piece of thick brown paper. Bea looked fearfully around the room, but the drunk was still sleeping and the little chef had returned to the kitchen. Darlene had jumped up and was about to run out without her coat. "Darlene!" Bea cried— "God damn it! . . . get your coat!"

The man in flight now thrust his right hand menacingly in his jacket pocket. His eyes took on a maniacal glitter as he watched Darlene struggle into her coat. Then suddenly he lunged and seized her by the wrist with his other hand. "Wait a minute!" he breathed. "I'm going with you two. . . . And don't start anything!" Then he turned her loose, got in his overcoat, and grabbed up the package. "Okay! Okay!" he said. "Go ahead! . . . lead and I'll follow you! Go *on!*" He glared at Bea and put his free right hand threateningly in his jacket pocket again. "Sure!" he exulted —"I'm going home with you! I only need a little time— just a couple of weeks to keep low. . . . that's all I need! The police have not found out yet—it's only been a few hours. But when they do, later on today, they'll be expecting me to blow town—won't they? So I've got to get lost for a few days!—right here in town! Okay, okay!—go on ahead! And don't try anything!"

Frightened Darlene looked at Bea. But Bea now stood strangely transfigured. It was as if some brand new—heaven-sent—thought had hit her. Musing, crafty, she bit her lip as she watched him.

But soon the three of them were out in the street. It was still snowing lightly as Bea led the way to her car—an old second-hand crimson Cadillac—parked a half block down from the cafeteria. She thrust a stick of chewing gum in her mouth as she batted her eyes against the falling flakes, then unlocked the right front door of the car.

"Get in," she told him. "Darlene, you set in the back." Then unobtrusively she slipped Darlene her purse. When Darlene got in the back seat and opened the purse, she saw Bea's tiny pearl-handled revolver.

It was 7:40 as they pulled away from the curb. Though the morning had grown lighter, the air was full of smoke belching from the chimneys of nearby apartment buildings. It flew in all directions, mingling with the falling snow and giving it a sickening, acrid smell. The man in flight, his breathing heavy, excited, sat beside Bea with his package in his lap.

When they had gone about two blocks, Bea glanced over her shoulder. "Okay, Darlene," she said, "show him what you got."

He turned around. Darlene let him see the pistol. "Oh, God!" he said, panicking—and spun back around, gaping at Bea. "Let me out!" he pleaded. "Don't, don't take advantage of me! Oh, come on, let me out! ..."

Bea, turning a corner, frowned. "Take it easy, now," she warned, "if you don't want me to drive to the police station with you. And keep your hands in your lap. Darlene, see what *he's* got. Don't miss nothing. Watch him, now—be careful."

Darlene looked frightened, shocked. She hesitated. "Bea, you're nuts!" she said. "I'm onto you.... *I* know what you got in mind."

"You do, do you?" Bea said grimly. "Well, God damn it, act like it, then!"

"... Is this a miserable stick-up?" the anguished man in flight asked. "What is it? ... Let me out of here, will you? It's a stick-up and—"

Bea kept driving. "No, it ain't a stick-up," she said. "We just wanta check your hardware."

"Then, you're going to turn me in, that's it! ... for a reward!"

"Not *you,* my friend," said Bea. "Hurry up, Darlene—see what he's got."

Darlene, shaking her head, muttering, leaned over the front seat and methodically went through his pockets, but found no weapons.

"So you was bluffin' us," Bea said to him. "What'd you do with the knife, then? *Some* knife—Jesus! It musta almost been an ax."

He sat very straight, shuddering. "I threw it away—out the taxi window. . . . coming through the park."

"What's your name?"

". . . Yeager. . . . Jackson Yeager."

"What you do for a living?"

". . . I was in religious work."

"In *what*?" Bea turned and stared incredulously. "Is that how you learned to drink whiskey and use a knife? Whatta you mean 'religious work?' "

"I worked for the Black Christian Publishing Company . . . on their editorial staff. I did a column on New Testament interpretations — and wrote inspirational articles sometimes."

Bea took a deep breath and kept driving. "Are you from around town here?"

"No . . . we came—" His lip quivered and he could not go on. He closed his eyes. "My wife and I came here . . . about two years ago," he finally said. "We came from New Waterford."

"Well, you're in a brand new ball game now," Bea told him. "You just got through shanghaiin' your own self." She turned and looked at him again. "He ain't bad lookin', either, Darlene. May be a little thin—but a real clean-cut, nice-lookin', brown-skin man. How old are you, Jackson?"

". . . I'll soon be forty."

Darlene spoke up disgustedly. "Bea, do you know what you're doin'? This guy's gotta be crazy—insane! . . . he's a mental case! After what he did—Christ! You ain't forgot, have you, what he's holding there in his lap."

"No, I ain't forgot—I'm taking care of that now." Bea turned to Jackson Yeager to explain. "We're on our way 'cross town—to the river bridge. When we get there, if there ain't any cars coming, you're gonna get out and throw your wife's head in the river. If there is a car coming, then we're gonna circle the block and come back, time and again if we have to, 'til you get rid of it."

He shuddered again. His lips began moving as if in self-communion or silent prayer.

Soon they were out of the ghetto section and heading west toward the river. Big wet snowflakes were sticking to the windshield and Bea started the erratic wipers. In a few minutes they passed two parked police cars in one of which a policeman sat eating a hamburger. "Looka there," Bea said to Yeager. "You're luckier'n hell. Suppose I pulled over and told 'em to come and take a look at your package? In less'n a half-hour's time they'd know the rest of the story—that you just cut a white man to death *too*. The prosecutin' attorney himself couldn't keep you from gettin' the 'lectric chair. I ain't gonna do that, though. I'm takin' you home with us. That's where you said you wanted to go, ain't it? But it'll be for longer'n any couple of weeks. I got plans for you. I can always finger you to the police, too, y'know—and I'd do it in a minute if you don't pan out. It's strictly up to you—what happens to you from here on is in your own hands."

His intense whispering had brought spittle to his lips. He gave her another wild, anguished look. "How . . . how am I supposed to know what you're talking about!" he said.

Bea nodded—"You'll find out."

Darlene, angry, nervous, upset, stared straight ahead between them through the windshield. Soon they were going through a part of the business district, still headed west. Fifteen minutes later they approached the river bridge—a medium-sized modern span—as Bea hawked and spat out her window. "We gotta keep our eyes open, now," she warned them. "When we first get on the bridge we'll let him out, and he can walk across. We'll wait for him on the other side. Jackson, don't try to make a break and get away, now, because I'll have a dozen squad cars around you before you get three blocks. Okay—and make sure there ain't nobody looking when you throw that thing over. You bungle this and you're in trouble. All right—

get ready! Anybody back of us, Darlene?"

Darlene, muttering again, turned around and looked out the rear window. "It's clear," she said. "Bea, you've lost *your* mind, too."

Bea, heedless, grim, drove onto the bridge and stopped. For a moment Yeager froze. She frowned at him, and he looked piteously at her. Then, struggling, holding the package, he finally climbed out of the car and started trotting and stumbling along the pedestrian walkway of the bridge. The women drove on toward the other side. When he was nearly halfway across, he looked fearfully behind, ahead, and around him, then went to the railing and made a limp move to throw the package over. He could not. He seemed crazed, possessed, as he crushed the package closer to him and walked fifteen feet farther. Again he turned to the railing. But once more hesitated. He stood staring down at the dark, swirling waters. Yet at last, slowly, as if performing a ritual, he raised the package and held it out for a moment, then let it fall over the railing. He stood there. It seemed he would not move. But finally he turned and stumbled ahead toward the waiting car. When he rejoined the women and they all drove off, instead of tears he wiped clear dripping mucus from his nose with the back of his hand. Meanwhile Bea was heading the old Cadillac back toward the ghetto and home.

Chapter 2

THE ride back took twenty minutes. The temperature had climbed a few degrees, and the thin wet snow was a dirty grey. Darlene, worried and morose, stared out in silence at the passing city sights, while Yeager sat limp in the front seat. All the way Bea was businesslike, brusque, and preoccupied, though in the last five minutes of the trip she talked of the coming evening.

"We gotta be ready early," she told Darlene. "There'll be a mob tonight."

"Yeah," Darlene said.

"Remind me to call up and get a case of club soda and a half case of Scotch. I got enough of everything else, I think. They seem to be drinkin' more Scotch, don't they? No beer much any more. It used to be bourbon—maybe a little Scotch—but mostly beer, remember? We're gettin' more quality people, that's why. But, hell, what's Kalandyk care?—he don't give a damn one way or the other, because he made just as much off a bottle of beer as he does now off a shot of Scotch. Ha, it ain't sellin' no damn drinks *he's* interested in—it's what they pay at the door to get in that keeps him happy."

Yeager aroused himself once and gave Bea a bleary,

mystified look, then lapsed into his torpor again.

As they reentered the ghetto there were more people on the streets than earlier and more furnace smoke in the air. Soon Darlene was coughing. "Put your window up, Bea," she said. Bea closed her window, and at once the heater made it insufferable inside the smelly old car. Yeager sat mute, inert, gazing through the windshield.

At last they arrived in front of a big, drab, three-story apartment building. Bea parked and turned off the motor, then looked at Yeager when he made no move to get out. "Okay," she said—"This is the end of the line."

They all got out and Yeager followed them up the stairs of the building to the top floor. There Darlene used three keys to unlock the heavy door, and went in first. Bea stepped aside to let him enter next, and as he passed her she gave him a curious, hard-eyed stare from head to foot. When they were inside and the door was closed and carefully locked again, he seemed to come more to life, and turned and stared all about him.

He stood in a large entrance hall with faded, ornate columns. It appeared at one time to have been a kind of grand foyer. Ahead, slightly on the right of the foyer, there was a small bar for serving drinks. The apartment was very large, and now seamy-looking, yet decades ago had doubtless been occupied by well-to-do whites before their exodus. Directly off the foyer, and also on the right, was a huge room that could formerly have been a drawing room, and was entered through tall, massive double doors that now stood wide open. The room was almost square, and its expanse of parquet floor, except for one spot, was uncarpeted. It now seemed to be some kind of an arena. Around all four walls there were makeshift, but sturdy tiers, mounted with seats—stools, benches, chairs—three rows high, with a total seating capacity of from eighty to a hundred people. But the space down in the center, the well, of the arena was small, barely accommodating its little nine by six frayed carpet. A single electric light bulb, attached below a green porcelain shade, dangled directly over the carpet—the spot on which stood a cot with mattress.

Yeager, looking, suddenly intent, somehow felt in awe of the room. There was also fear, unintelligible fear. But now Bea, at his elbow, was pointing in another direction —to his left, down an interminably long hall running to the very rear of the apartment. "Go straight back," she said, and followed him. Darlene had pressed the button that sent on the cloudy hall lights and was already half-way down the hall—along both sides of which were many bedrooms, with a large dining room and the kitchen in the rear. Darlene kept walking until she turned into the last bedroom on the right, and Bea soon showed him into the one directly opposite it.

Bea flicked on the light, and the room was at once unattractive. It was plain, almost bare, with the pink plaster walls grimy and peeling in places. The light Bea had just put on, the only one in the room, an ancient cherubic Florentine fixture, was in the center of the ceiling and glaring bright. The only floor covering was a dingy scatter rug by the side of the bed.

Bea leaned against the foot of the bed as disheveled Yeager stood ineptly before her. She studied him for a moment, then yawned. "Well, get yourself some sleep," she said. "Christ, you look wild. As soon as I can, I'll see about gettin' you some other clothes, so we can burn them bloody things you got on. Meantime, take it easy right here in your room. Here's somethin' I want you to get straight, though: You can't slip outa this house and get away with it. You better believe me. I'd have the police on you so quick it'd make your head swim—you'd be in Canton Street jail in thirty minutes. Remember that. So relax. I'm puttin' a TV set in here for you, and you'll get good food here, too. Nobody's gonna hurt you, so stop lookin' so wild and scared—after what you just pulled, this is the safest place you could be right now. So get yourself together. I'll make you one promise: As long as you're in my house, the police'll never get you. That's a promise. In a day or two, when you get kinda settled, I'll tell you what this place here is all about and why I brought you here." She pointed at the wall—"There's a bathroom right there, the next room, and another one still farther up the hall. When you wake up, if you're hungry, you can go back there in the kitchen and see old Jessie. She's my cook— she'll feed you." Bea sized him up again for a moment, and seemed on the verge of talking more. But instead, yawning again, she soon left and closed the door behind her.

He stood in the middle of the room and for a moment stared at the door. Finally he got out of his overcoat and hung it and his hat in the musty closet, then sat down in the straightback chair, the only chair in the room, and began unloosening his shoe laces. Suddenly, he thrust forward in the chair, plunged his head in his hands, and emitted a low, guttural moan. But soon he stared out the window at the wet snow coming down onto the roofs of the other run-down apartment buildings. The back lots abutted on an unsightly alley and the rear stairs of the building next door were quilted with a sooty slush. At last he got up and inspected the bed. It was an ancient object, with a faded spread and creaky springs, but the linen was fresh. The old dresser opposite it had three drawers which were empty now and lined with newspapers brittle with age. The little table, almost behind the door, had legs so frail it appeared to require the wall for support. There was an ash tray on it and a 15¢ comic book, and the straightback chair beside it seemed the sturdiest piece in the room. He sat down on the bed and tried to slow his cataracting thoughts, his mystification, his fright. Yet there was almost no sensation of the passing of time. As he lay back wearily on the pillow to try to quell the tumult in his head, he realized the extent of his exhaustion, and soon began to feel slowly weightless, as if suspended, or floating in the ether of an interminable fantasy . . . a ghastly dream. . . .

* * * * * *

That afternoon he was catapulted to a sitting position on the bed by the three bold knocks on his door. Except for his shoes he was fully dressed but could not remember where he was. His head throbbed from the sudden jolt of awaking, and his mouth was dry. Then Bea opened the door and came in, and he remembered. He had not meant to fall asleep, and now jerked his wristwatch up before his filmy eyes. It was 3:30. He leapt to his feet and stared around him.

Bea was in mules and a pink dressing gown. "Cool it, cool it," she said. "Well, every damn radio and TV in town's blaring it out. Christ Almighty, that was one of the biggest white men around here—it's all they're talkin' about, nothin' else. They found 'em about noon—the hotel maids found 'em."

He took the news glumly, stoically, and sat down on the bed again. Soon he began trying to identify, isolate, the fearful aching in his lower forehead, the forward skull, and concluded it was directly in back of the eyeballs, where the area was raw, excoriated, from his sense of the abrupt, evil presence of Bea. And the pink dressing gown —it made her seem bigger, hulkier, more masculine than ever, now that she came and stood over him, looming like a great cloud.

"All I can figure is, you musta been temporarily insane," she said. "You had to be, to do what you did. My God, and to carry that thing around, that awful thing, wrapped up just like it was a head of cabbage or somethin'. And then to show it to *us*!—a couple of rank strangers you just run into in a damn restaurant. . . . You had to be crazy! What'n the world happened?"

He only stared out the window and said nothing.

"Okay. But there's one thing you gotta do, and that is get yourself a new name. They're scourin' this town for you—you're the husband, y'know—and all the people here in the house listen to radio and TV and read the papers, and they'll hear or see your name. You gotta get a new name. How 'bout somethin' like Smith? Or Carter, maybe. Yeah, William Carter. Sure—Willie."

He looked at her for a moment, then took a deep breath. "Whatever you say," he finally nodded. ". . . I've got a little money on me—I can pay something for staying here a few days."

"Now wait," she said. "Let's don't get started on that. I didn't say nothin' about money. I didn't say nothin' about a 'few days,' either. In fact, I said just the opposite. As far as money's concerned, I may be payin' *you* before it's over."

He looked at her in bewilderment. His lips parted once, but he did not speak.

She changed the subject. "Bismarck, my bartender, is roundin' up some clean clothes for you, and a razor and a toothbrush and some things. He'll bring the TV in too pretty soon and you can stay in your room tonight and take it easy. I'll get a sandwich to you after while, but tomorrow we'll all be eatin' in the dining room, and you'll get to meet everybody then." She gathered her flowing pink dressing gown about her and stood watching him for a moment. Finally she left.

He sat there for awhile, but soon lay back feebly on the bed again. When he found he could no longer sleep, he got up and stood at the window, gazing down on the unsightly alley. The snow and rain had stopped but the skies were still a leaden grey. Time dragged. He tried to think, but with little success. It seemed his mind only functioned in relation to certain stimuli and was blocked off against others, until at last he found himself across the room, sitting in the chair wringing his hands. An hour and a half passed. Then a rowdy March wind rose and came in against the windows, rattling the panes and the corrugated metal roof on the little one-car garage below.

At 5:45 it was getting dark, when there was another knock on his door. He opened it to an old man, in his late sixties, with parchmentlike brown skin and wooly hair, almost white. He had brought two laundered shirts, a pair of trousers, and some toilet articles. "Howdy," he said, but did not smile. "Bea sent these." He put everything down on the bed as he sniffed disdainfully at the closeness of the room. Pointing to the trousers, he added, "These're a little long for you, but they'll do 'til we can get somethin' better." He studied Yeager for a moment, then stepped back toward the door.

"Thanks," Yeager finally said. "Are you Bismarck?"

"Yes."

"Have . . . have you got a Bible you could let me have for a little while?"

The old man stared at him. "A Bible? . . . No, I ain't got a Bible. Ain't had one for years." He left.

Yeager went in the adjacent bathroom and washed and shaved. When he returned he discarded his sullied clothing in a closet corner and put on the trousers Bismarck had brought, turning up the cuffs, and one of the clean shirts. He sat languishing in his room until almost 7:00 before vaguely realizing he was waiting for the food Bea had promised. But none came. Then, about 7:30, he became aware of a growing, bustling, activity throughout the apartment. The place had come alive—he could hear talking, bath water running, and a stir of commotion in the rooms along the hall. Also, someone was playing blues and hot jazz on a small phonograph somewhere up front, and soon, past his door, there was much hurried coming and going in the hall. He could sense lively preparation for some major event, and remembered Bea's talk in the car about the evening to come. He sat very still under the brazen ceiling light, trying to fathom what was happening. Soon he heard someone carrying bottles and tinkling glassware up the hall. He recalled the bar and Bea's remarks about the sale of liquor, and thought of old Bismarck, the bartender. Now he heard Bea's heavy voice back in the kitchen, giving orders, and also someone laughing in Darlene's room directly across the hall.

Finally, a few minutes after 8:00, the loud doorbell up front sounded for the first time. At once someone hurried, almost ran, up the hall to buzz the callers up. Intermittent rings then followed only two or three minutes apart, and soon there was much movement, talk, and merrymaking up in the foyer by the increasing number of arriving guests. He strained to hear, and could detect they were both men and women and by their speech were white people. He was mystified. The noise grew in volume as time went on and the number of guests increased, until by 9:00 there was such a swell of voices and milling around that he sensed the foyer was crowded and that much drinking was going on.

Fully dressed, he lay down on his back across the bed and, fixing his eyes on the horrid light above him, listened with pounding heart. By 9:15 the noise had reached the peak of an hour-long crescendo. But at last now it began to ebb, subside, become sporadic chatter, until within minutes a strange, hushed, forbidding silence had come. The guests all seemed to have dissolved, or gone somewhere—moved into another room with doors heavy enough to seal in the sound. He remembered the arena.

He sprang off the bed, went to his door, and put his ear against it to listen. But heard nothing. He stood there for five minutes. Yet only silence. At last he lay down again and stared at the light. For the next hour the front of the apartment was deathly still. The only sounds came from the rear, the kitchen, where someone was washing dishes or glasses. Time seemed interminable; it was like the whole night had passed.

Finally at 10:20, as if great doors had been flung wide, he heard the rolling, swelling, surging sound again. He quickly sat up, straining once more to hear. The crowd was returning, spilling back into the foyer—it seemed all of them at once, for he sensed the same heavy pressure of numbers as before. Then he heard someone running down the hall toward him—a woman, who, as she ran, was laugh-

ing and cursing in filthy obscenities. Suddenly he realized
it was Darlene. He leapt off the bed again, ran to his door,
and cracked it just in time to glimpse her as she whisked
into her room and slammed her door. But he had seen that
she was barefoot and wore only a kimono. Now, as he
slowly closed his door, he heard the crowd up front leaving
at last—pushing, shoving, laughing its way out Bea's front
door. He felt a strange sense of terror.

About a half hour later there was a rude kick on his
door, before Bea's voice came through. "Open the door—
I got my hands full!" He let her in. She entered carrying
a roast beef sandwich and two dill pickles on a plate in one
hand and a cold can of beer in the other. Pinioned under
her left arm was the evening's newspaper. He stared at her
—she was wearing a huge, flowing red wig. And her low-
cut silver dress was only a foil for the gaudy costume
jewelry and the oyster-white satin pumps. As soon as she
put the food and beer down on the little table, she tossed
the newspaper on the bed. "Read it and weep," she said.

His trembling hand picked up the newspaper as the
headline jumped at him: "NOEL RUPERT SLAIN IN
HOTEL TRYST!" The subhead of the story ran: "Black
Woman's Head Hacked Off. Husband Sought." He turned
his head away and put the paper down.

"Y'might as well go on and read it," she said. "I know
it's like takin' bad medicine, all right. You kin see now,

though, can't you, how lucky you are to be in here off the street. Every damn gendarme on the force is turnin' this town upside down and inside out lookin' for you." She pointed to the newspaper again. "Go ahead—read the rest."

Instead he looked at her. "Will you tell me why you brought me here?" he said at last.

"Now, now, I ain't gonna get into that yet. You'll find out soon enough."

His anger suddenly flared. "What do you take me for! ... some kind of blockhead! What's all this about? ... why did you bring me here? I'm entitled to know!"

"You're entitled to shit! Don't hand me that! Yeah, you're entitled to the 'lectric chair, all right. *I'm* the one that asks the questions around here! ... everybody else answers 'em!—you'll find that out!" She left.

Breathing hard, he sat down at once and read the whole news story. The police had been quick, he saw. Already the bellboy had confessed to taking his twenty dollars to sneak out a key to the room Rupert kept at this very ordinary hotel for his dalliances—including that with Florrie Yeager.

He soon sat munching the sandwich and sipping the beer—thinking hard, striving to repossess himself. In back of his eyeballs the pain still ground and throbbed as he tried to unravel the tangle of all he had seen and heard in this bizarre house that was now both his refuge and prison.

Chapter 3

H E awoke the next morning, Thursday, at 7:30 craving a cigarette. He had not smoked since coming there, had strangely had no desire to, although he ordinarily smoked at least a pack a day. He had been afraid to undress the night before and had slept on top of the covers in his clothing with his overcoat thrown over him. Now he sat up and fumbled in his pockets until he found his cigarettes and sat on the side of the bed smoking. Afterwards he gathered up his toilet articles, went in the bathroom, and locked the door. As he viewed himself in the mirror, he estimated he had lost at least fifteen pounds within two weeks, and the brown skin of his face was rough, welty, and drawn; his eyes empty. He had brushed his teeth and was splashing cold water on his face, when suddenly he heard someone trying the bathroom doorknob. He turned and saw the knob twisting violently. Fear stirred in his stomach.

"I'm coming out," he called, his voice hoarse, and at once wiped his face and retrieved his toilet articles. Yet, the person outside began angrily jerking and shaking the knob, and when at last he unlocked and opened the door, he was met with the baleful stare of a child—a little black girl, hardly eight years old, who now glowered at him.

"Who're *you?*" she asked. She wore tiny cotton pajamas, and her hair was in a dozen little pigtails. "What you doin' in our bathroom?"

He stammered his answer. "I'm . . . I'm living here." Then he sidled past her into the hall, and she was still glaring at him as he went in his room.

Almost immediately he heard Bea out in the hall scolding the child. "Iris!—you mind your own damn bussiness! Go in that bathroom and brush your teeth and get outa here to school."

"He went in *there,* Mama!—in Chester's room! What's he doin' in Chester's room?"

"It's none of your business what he's doin' in there! You better listen to me, Iris!—keep on, and you're gonna get your little butt whipped again!" Bea returned to her room.

. . . Ah, Bea's child, he mused. What a brat. But who was Chester? . . .

Nine o'clock came. Still no one else in the house was up. He decided to go to the kitchen and forage for coffee. The sky had cleared during the night and when, for the first time, he entered the kitchen, the sun was level with the tops of the buildings and streaming in at the windows. The big stove was old and blackened from use, but the linoleum looked new and the chairs were chromium and modern. On the large wall opposite the stove there was a glass-doored cupboard reaching almost to the ceiling, containing dozens of glasses of all shapes and sizes and various brands of whiskey. Next to the teakettle on the back of the stove he saw the coffee pot and soon found a can of ground coffee in a smaller cupboard beneath the liquor. In a few minutes he had brewed coffee and sat at the kitchen table, a full cup in hand.

Then he heard someone coming down the hall toward him. His heart began pounding again. He looked nervously about him but kept his seat. The approaching footsteps were light and languid—too light for Bea's and coming from too great a distance for Darlene's. Soon a pudgy, light brown-skinned young man entered the kitchen. He wore suede loafers, cinnamon slacks, and a fawn cashmere sweater. Before seeing Yeager he had absently touched his pile of hair, which, though worn natural, had been color-rinsed a light copper. Yeager stared at him. The young man, when he saw Yeager, stopped short and, surprised, stared back. Then his face lit up in a smile of greeting. "Oh, hello, there!" he sang.

Finally Yeager nodded. ". . . Good morning."

"It *is* a good morning!" The young man's voice trailed in a high soprano as he crossed the room to the stove. He gently shook the teakettle, refilled it under the tap, and with a fastidious wrist action, placed it on the burner. Then, smiling, he turned to Yeager again. "Are you living here?" he asked, in the lyric tone.

Yeager first had to clear his throat. ". . . Yes," he said, and brought up his cup as his eyes sped away.

The young man took a tea bag out of a jar in the cupboard and retreated to a tall stool across the kitchen from Yeager. As he sat waiting for the water to boil, he dangled the tea bag at the end of its string in his manicured hand and, occasionally, knowingly, glancing at Yeager, whistled softly. His face, even though now relaxed, was desperate, grotesque, its brown color whitish and washed-out as if from use of skin bleach or white powder. Now he glanced toward the door and laughed. "Bea's sure sleeping late today. But this is always a lazy house in the morning."

". . . She was up earlier," Yeager finally ventured— "with the little girl."

"Oh, Iris! Yes, Iris is up every morning like clockwork, all by herself—especially when Bea's been up late or has got a big head. Ha, ha, ha!" They sat in silence for a moment as he continued twirling the tea bag. Then he smiled, again knowingly—"Are you going to be with us?"

Yeager hesitated, and looked warily at him. ". . . Yes, I'll be living here. . . . I'll be here for a little while, at least. . . ."

"Oh, swell!" Beaming, the young man immediately

scooted his soft round hips down off the stool and came over and shook Yeager's hand—"My name's Donald. Wonderful!—we'll be seeing a lot of each other, then. What's your name?"

Yeager dropped the limp hand. ". . . Bill Carter," he finally said, and swallowed.

"Hello, Bill!" Donald, still beaming, stood over him for a moment, then, his back arched sharply, returned to the stove and made and poured his tea. Soon, holding the cup and saucer precariously as he prepared to go, he paused and gave his knowing smile once more. "You know," he whispered, "Bea's been trying like mad to find another guy somewhere for her setup here. She's probably told you about Chester. He walked out on us—didn't say a word, just up and disappeared. She's been beside herself ever since—frantic to find somebody to take his place. I hope you'll like it. We have some great—oh, exciting!— times around here!" He gave his high lilting laugh again, a manicured wave, and left with his tea.

Yeager only sat there. Even later when he returned to his room he could only stand staring bewilderedly at the bare walls. Finally, he sat in the chair and, lapsing into a deep, questioning study, rubbed his knuckles and murmured to himself. Soon all the nightmarish fear had returned, and he held his head and began moaning again.

At 10:30 that morning Darlene came to his room.

He started at her knock, and jumped up. She wore her coat, as if on her way out, and had brought him some crackers and an orange. "This is the only food in the house right now," she said, viewing him guardedly. "You're probably starved, but we'll have a big feed this evenin', in the dining room." She stood in the door, anxiety on her face, and stared at his hollow eyes.

Somehow sensing her compassion, he suddenly seized her by the arm and pulled her inside. "Sit down! . . . Oh, please sit down!" he breathed, closing the door. "Can I talk to you? . . . only for a minute!" He turned her loose and, taking the orange and crackers from her, peered into her face again.

She quickly stepped back from him. "I can't now—I gotta go out!"

"Please! . . . When will you be back? I've got to talk to you—or somebody!"

". . . I'll be back by dinnertime," she said, frightened. Already she had opened the door, and now she hurried out.

At once, voraciously, he began eating the crackers, then he peeled the orange and gulped it in quarters. But soon he was pacing the floor and, although he kept telling himself he must not panic, he felt any minute he would collapse, disintegrate. Again he tried to sort out and arrange the facts as best he understood them, but only confusion resulted, and time dragged.

Finally by mid-afternoon the house began to stir, and at 3:30 Iris came home from school—he could hear her running down the hall. And soon now he caught the wafting smells of food, of chicken frying in the kitchen, and far up the hall the little phonograph was going again. Then came scattered talk and laughter from some of the closer rooms, and he realized there were many people living in the house. Ten minutes later someone knocked. He thought of Darlene and sprang at the door.

Instead it was old Bismarck again. He had brought a portable television set. "How'ya doin'?" he panted, frowning as usual, as he stepped in with it—he wore a dark blue serge suit, shiny from wear, and a starched white shirt and necktie. "I'm bringing you my prize pleasure," he said, setting the television on the shaky little table. "Yeah, I'm givin' it up, I guess. It's been a world of company, though—but I'm turnin' it over to you now. Lord, will I miss it. I looked at the movies."

Yeager glanced at the television. "I didn't ask for it," he said glumly.

"Oh, I brought it on orders of the queen Bea herself," Bismarck grinned, petulantly, showing his ill-fitting dentures. "It belongs to her—she's been lettin' me use it, that's all. She's got a big color set up in her room. Wouldn't it be dandy to have one of them—Lord!" He spread the V-shaped aerial and adjusted it. "You plannin' to be here quite some time, probably," he said—"or else I might be gettin' it back before long, huh?"

Yeager hesitated. ". . . I don't know yet. But—"

"—You're takin' Chester's place, ain't you? . . ."

At that moment little Iris came in the room, both arms piled high with more clothing for Yeager—socks, underwear, another shirt, a sweater, a pair of grey slacks, a robe, and a motley blue jacket. She tossed them on the bed contemptuously and marched out.

"Bea had me pick 'em up for you today," Bismarck said, pointing with condescension. "She said you been kinda down on your luck."

Yeager glowered. "What else did she tell you?"

"Your name—Willie Carter—and that you was gonna be stayin' here in Chester's room." Bismarck grinned again, knowingly, as he moved backward to the door. "I gotta go now and help out Jessie in the kitchen—that old gal's cooked a fine dinner back there. We'll be eatin' before long." He left.

Yeager went in the bathroom and bathed, shaved, and put on clean clothing. At 5:30 Darlene came to his room again. "Dinner's about ready," she said. "You can come with me if you want to." She wore a blouse with a ruffle front and a very short skirt, and her heavy eyebrow make-up made her look older, more hardened, as she stood in his door.

Again he tried to get her to come in. "Please, Darlene!" he whispered. "Can I talk to you for a minute before we go?....only a minute! I want to ask you..."

"I can't talk now." She drew back from him, shaking her head. "... not right now, anyhow." She looked furtively up the hall. "But I'd sure tell you to get outa here, to leave this house—and the sooner the better. Come on, let's go to the dinin' room."

He stood staring. But at last he followed her.

They entered the dining room. It was large, old-fashioned, and drab, with the elongated dining table covered with a coffee-stained, rose tablecloth. There was a massive old sideboard on the longer wall and a slime-murky tank of goldfish across on the other. Also, on a shelf attached to the shorter wall rested four potted plants.

Darlene was pensive, preoccupied, as she walked ahead of him partway around the table, where a tall, thin octoroon woman—in her middle thirties, and pale and sickly-looking—was going around the table in the opposite direction placing down silverware and paper napkins.

"Cleo," Darlene said to her, "you ain't met Willie, here, yet, have you?—Willie Carter?"

"No, I ain't," Cleo grinned. "But I sure have heard about him." Her voice was raucous and hoarse, as if from abusive use of whiskey and cigarettes. "Welcome, Willie.

You're just in time to be my dinner partner. Set here."
She laughed and patted the back of a chair midway the
table.

Yeager finally went around and stood at the place, but
soon caught Darlene watching him with worried, furtive,
possessive eyes.

"And stay away from that Darlene," Cleo said mockingly. "She's got many a man in trouble. So watch her."

Darlene smiled but ignored Cleo's quips.

Iris came in now carrying a plate of corn muffins, which
she put on the edge of the table. Suddenly Bea's drunken
voice came out of the kitchen, followed by her coarse,
deriding laugh. Cleo gave a hacking cough into her fist.
"Bea's hangin' one on today," she said to Darlene—"She's
drinkin' rum, of all things. You know what that does to
her." She placed down the last napkin, turned, and gave
Yeager a quizzical look. "Willie, if you ask me, you don't
look so hot—so happy. What's the matter? You ain't
always like this, I hope, are you?"

He gave her a wary glance, hesitated, then said nothing.

She coughed deeply, hard, again. For a moment her face
was livid. At last she pushed her long hair back behind her
ears and he saw her emaciated arms and the myriad rings
on her white bony fingers. "What's the matter with him,
Darlene?" she said. "He ain't gonna let us down like
Chester did, is he?" She clapped her hand to her mouth—

"*Oh*, maybe I'm talkin' out of school."

Yeager, his lips parted, stared at her.

Darlene grinned—"Cleo, you're smokin' that pot again, ain't you?"

Cleo disregarded the remark. "Oh, but what the hell," she said, "Chester and Donald wasn't gettin' along so hot anyhow. You remember that fight—ha, that hair-pullin' contest—they had here one night." She looked at Yeager. "Willie ain't met Donald yet, has he? Oh, but he will!" She gave her coarse laugh, then went into another coughing fit.

Old Bismarck, wearing an apron, brought in a huge platter of fried chicken now and set it in the middle of the table. "Go round 'em up, Cleo!" he cried. "Hurry, hurry—'fore this food gits cold. We're ready! Where's everybody? Go git em, Cleo! Where's Mack? Where's Mavis? And Donald! Where *are* they, girl?"

"Oh, for Pete's sake, Bismarck, shut up," Cleo said. But she had started out of the room—when Donald entered.

"Oh, am I late?" he sang, touching his high, bronzed natural. Then he saw Yeager and stopped in his tracks. "Bill!" he said. ". . . oh, hi, Bill," his voice fell meltingly. Cleo threw her head back and laughed. Donald studied Yeager for a long moment before at last looking around self-consciously at the others.

"I see you two *have* met," Cleo said. "Well, that's

good." She went out.

"Are you about getting settled okay, Bill?" Donald asked with deepest solicitude. "If you need anything, just holler." He still wore his suede loafers and cinnamon slacks, this time with a pearl-grey jacket and ascot scarf.

Suddenly Yeager was writhing. Darlene saw him and a stricken look came on her face.

Soon Cleo returned with a squat, burly fellow whom she introduced to Yeager as Mack Thomas. He was very dark, almost black, and about twenty-eight or nine. He wore tight corduroy pants, a polo shirt, and heavy side-burns down his cheeks. "Mack is God's gift to women *now*," Cleo wryly explained to Yeager, "but I learned him everything he knows."

"Ooo-la-la!" caroled Donald—"and that's a lot, sweetheart!"

Mack stood surveying the table, his hammy hands partially down in his tight pants pockets. "Fried chicken, eh?" he grunted. ". . . Not bad—not bad, man. Come on, then, let's git with it." He looked around at them and grinned —"After that deal last night, I *need* some proteins. And still them pecks was settin' up there droolin' for more, and still more. You can't satisfy 'em, man. Ain't they weird? And Mavis, she makes it worse. Wouldn't she?—showin' off all the time. And more'n ever now—since they got her believin' she's the star. It sure makes it hard on *me*. She's a little chick, all right, but tough as hell—strong, got stayin' power. It's all I can do to handle her sometimes. And then Cleo and Darlene after that. *Whew!* I'm ruinin' my health in this pad, man. Come on, let's eat." He sat down at the table.

"Oh, Lord," Cleo grinned, "Mack's feelin' sorry for himself again. Tsk, tsk! Mack's got it tough, ain't he? Poor Mack—he don't like his job. Like hell," she sneered.

Donald squealed with laughter.

Darlene looked distressed, in pain, as she glanced at Yeager, who stood open-mouthed.

Soon Iris and Bismarck brought in more food. Jessie, the cook, a toothless, snuff-dipping crone with a bad limp, came in from the kitchen now and inspected the table. "You ain't brought the gravy in yet, Iris," she scolded. "Hurry up, baby, and go git the gravy."

Suddenly Bea loomed in the doorway. She held a dark highball in her hand. "Where'n the hell's Mavis?" she demanded unsteadily, then sipped the drink again. She wore a sleeveless house dress, revealing her huge dark arms to the shoulders, and her protuberant lips were heavily lipsticked carmine. "Where's *Mavis*, I said!" She weaved over to the sideboard.

"Mavis is comin'!" an approaching voice, small and feminine, called from out in the hall. Then a very pretty, petite, black girl hurried in. Her figure was firm and curvaceous, yet lithe, and the features of her ebony face were as perfect as if machine-made.

Bea, leaning against the sideboard, drunkenly ogled her —and summoned her with her drink. "Come over here, you fine little filly, you."

Mavis giggled warily. "Look out, now, Bea—no rough stuff," she said, and went instead around to the far side of the table. There Cleo introduced her to Yeager.

But Bea soon lost interest and began frowning around the room, as if counting heads. She cried back to the kitchen—"Okay, you-all! Come on, *lessss eat!*"

Bismarck, Iris, and old Jessie soon came in and everyone sat down at the table—ten in all. Bea, highball still in hand, dropped heavily into her chair at the head of the table and looked down at Bismarck seated to the left of shapely Mavis. "Okay, Bismarck, say the blessin'," she said.

Bismarck bowed his head, closed his eyes, and mumbled a short prayer. Then the loaded serving dishes went around from hand to hand and everyone took large helpings of the fried chicken, mashed potatoes with cream gravy, succotash, candied yams, salad, and corn muffins. Even Iris, seated at the foot of the table, had a heaping plate. Mack Thomas, sitting to the right of Mavis, had begun eating at once—greedily, noisily. Donald had early claimed the other chair beside Yeager, who sat next to Cleo, and was trying to draw him out in conversation. Yeager, though, was dour, mostly silent. Soon Mack looked pointedly across the table at him and said—"Say, how 'bout hearin' something from our new man, here. He ain't said three words all evenin'. Willie, tell us something 'bout yourself, man. You sure don't act like no damn playboy to me. Bea, does this cat look to you like a sure-nuff swinger? But maybe I oughta be askin' Donald *that*—Ha! Ha!"

Everyone got quiet.

"Now, *w-a-i-t* a minute!" Bea cried drunkenly, putting her drumstick down—"If he don't feel like talkin', that's his God-damn business, none of yours! Leave him alone, will'ya—stop pickin' on him!"

Cleo gave a quiet but cynical chuckle and said, "Well, Mack, you can sure tell he ain't no Chester."

"You damn right," Mack said.

"How d'you know?" Mavis tittered. "He just might make Chester look like a Sunday school teacher or somethin'. Right, Donald?"

Donald gave his high, fluttering laugh. "Ha-ha-ha!— you-all've got the floor, now. I ain't in this!"

"I said lay off him!" Bea bellowed.

"That's right!" Darlene said bitterly.

Donald, still smiling but now serious, spoke up. "From all I can see, Bill, here, is a real nice guy."

"Really?" Cleo grinned.

"Sure, he's quiet, but, ha, we got enough loudmouths

around here to make up for that. In the first place, Bea wouldn't have brought him here if he wasn't okay. Right, Bea, baby?"

Bea was staring down the table at them—"*S-a-y,* what got you-all on this subject, anyhow? You can all go to hell! . . . you're meddlin' in something that ain't none of your God-damn business!"

At this, Iris, down at the foot of the table, went into gales of laughter.

Bea gasped, then struggled halfway up out of her chair. "What *you* laughin' at, Iris? You don't know what we're talkin' about! All you're fixin' to do is get your little ass whipped again, like I been promisin' you to do all week! Another peep outa you and see if I don't." Reeking of rum, Bea now looked defiantly around the table at the others. "I said you-all're meddlin' in something that ain't none of your God-damn business!—d'you hear me?"

Finally Mavis bridled. "Well, if it ain't none of *our* business, I'd sure like to know whose it is!"

Bea's eyes went wide. "Look out, now!" she warned them all. "You're treadin' on dangerous ground. *I'm* runnin' this house, and don't any of you forget it. If you ever do, you know my remedy better'n I do. All I gotta do is so much as mention it to Bertie Kalandyk. You know that, don't you? 'Cause this is *his* investment. And he ain't gonna see it suffer, either, if you know Bertie, and except for Willie, everyone of you do. You're always talkin' about how Chester up and left. Well, you damn right he did. But do any of you know whatever happened to him? Of course you don't. All you can do is guess. The only thing any of us know is that Kalandyk was down on him because Chester fooled around so much, was gone from the house a lot, didn't always show up on time. Chester was like a damn kid—just happy-go-lucky. But that's all you know. And it's all I know, too. It's somethin' to think about, though, ain't it. *Ain't* it? You damn right it is! You don't think Kalandyk's givin' you his money for nothin', do you? He pays you damn good, and he ain't gonna take any of your lip—and neither *am I!* Now, I've heard enough of this bullshit—talk about somethin' else!" Bea reached and drained her highball glass.

The subject was dropped. Later, after huge slices of apple pie were served with coffee, they all dispersed.

Chapter 4

YEAGER returned to his room. Outside it was dark, but instead of putting on the blatant light, he went to the window and gazed out at the blackness sprinkled with the lights of the city. But the room soon grew eerie, and reluctantly he put on the light. Although his legs had gone weak again, he trembled no longer. A dull stoicism had come over him and deadened his senses, yet he had more than glimmerings of his catastrophe and strained to keep his mind far, far away. He did not succeed, for soon the slow aching fear returned and settled on him like a smothering mantle, starting him whispering to himself and pacing the floor again.

An hour later he was suddenly aware of the stillness throughout the apartment. Even all sounds of dishwashing had ceased. He concluded that soon after dinner almost everyone had gone out. No matter, he wanted to cross the hall and knock on Darlene's door—his urge to talk to her, question her, had become critical, a necessity. But finally he did not, convinced she too had gone. Nevertheless, in a few minutes he cracked his door and listened. Then he opened it enough to put his head out and look across the hall, then finally up the hall, where he could faintly hear a television in one of the rooms, though all the doors along the hall were closed and, up at the front end, the foyer was in solid darkness. After a moment he stepped from his room and very quietly went back to the kitchen— reconnoitering. There was no one there, and only one weak light on, over the sink. He tried the back door, but found it locked, impregnably—to insiders without the two keys as well as to outsiders—and both kitchen windows onto the back porch heavily barred, against burglaries. Soon he left the kitchen and started up the long, darkened hall.

When he finally reached the front—the foyer—he groped back and forth along the wall in the blackness until he found the light switch. The foyer, lighted, seemed to him even larger than on the morning of his arrival. He went over now and tried the big front door, but, as he expected, found it also heavily locked, in the same manner as in the kitchen. He thought of fire and shuddered. Next he turned around and, to the right as one entered the apartment, saw the bar again, and knew it was where Bismarck sold drinks. Then he noticed along the opposite wall the garment rack, long and sturdy, capable of accommodating scores of overcoats. And last, on the right and short of the bar, were the huge, tall double doors—into the arena.

The doors were closed, and when he tried the great knob he found they were locked. Suddenly in a fury, quivering, grating his teeth, he tried to wrench the knob off.

It of course would not give. He then put his frail, frenzied weight against the doors, but they remained mutely intact. Whereupon he stood glaring about him, embittered by his impotence. He was finally about to return to his room, when he saw, beyond the bar and a short distance past the slight curvature in the hallway, what might be a second, a rear, door to the arena. He went down at once and jerked it open. There was only a great cavern of blackness inside, a ringing silence, a musty smell. But he entered quickly, knowing it was the arena, and that he must stay close to the wall. He felt for a light switch, but, finding none, began groping his way along the wall back up in the direction of the locked double doors, under which he was soon able to see the strip of light from the foyer outside. He was more confident.

Then suddenly in the pitch black he collided with a heavy object. It made a loud noise as it hit the bare floor. His heart stopped, then began racing furiously, as he stood perfectly still for almost three minutes, waiting for some-one to come investigating. But when at last no one came, he felt around on the floor and picked the object up. It was some kind of marble sculpture—or bust. A head! His flesh went cold. Grimly, his fingers went over it, feeling the chin, the cheekbones, the hair, the dainty mouth—a woman! He stood holding it for a moment, trembling. But finally with great care he put it down against the wall

the hall watching him, and had seen it all.

He bellowed at her. *"What do you want!* . . . you . . . you little . . .!" He lunged at the doorway. But she ran— leaving him shaking. He slammed the door. Soon he lay down feebly across the bed again, closing his eyes against the horrid light. He would stay awake, he finally told himself, until Darlene came home. He *must* talk to her tonight. Yet, hours later, near midnight, he at last slipped into a troubled sleep with the light full in his face.

Much later that night he was awakened by someone in the bathroom. He sat up and squinted at his watch. It was a few minutes past three o'clock. As he stood up he heard the person leave the bathroom and enter the room across the hall, and he knew it was Darlene. He left his room at once and knocked on her door. She must have been doing something very near the door, for she opened it quickly, almost as if she had been expecting someone. She gaped when she saw who it was. She was fully dressed and had just come in—behind her he could see her coat thrown carelessly across a chair and partly on the floor. He could also see she had been drinking.

"Oh, no," she said with tipsy contempt, and walked away from the door.

"I know it's late," he said, "but could I talk to you for just a few minutes?—I won't keep you up."

"You damn right you won't." She picked up her coat

and, dragging it, weaved over to the closet and hung it up—speaking so thickly he had difficulty at first making out her words. "I'm tired," she said, "and I'm sleepy, and I don't wanta talk. Don't just stand there—close the door."

"Can I come in, then?"

"I don't care what you do. Just close that door—you wanta wake up everybody in the house?" She came back from the closet, sat down heavily on the bed, and kicked off her shoes. Wearing a short dress, she lifted one knee and unhooked a stocking from her garter panties—he could see the panties and the smooth brown flesh of her thighs. "I see you're still with us," she said. "Well, you won't be when you find out what the deal is. Ha!—you'll take your chances in the street and be glad."

He had closed the door. "That's what I wanted to talk to you about. There's no one I can talk to but you—you're my only friend here." He hesitated—"or any place. . . ." When she looked mockingly at him, he paused again. ". . . I feel that way, anyhow," he said.

She wore less make-up tonight, and to him seemed younger, more attractive. She had taken off both stockings, and now stood up, unzipped her dress in the back, and went over and took her robe out of the closet. Pushing her dress and slip off her shoulders, she worked them down past her oval hips and stepped out of them. He could smell the faintest body odor blended with her strong sweetish perfume and against all inclination his blood jumped. Now in only garter panties and brassiere, she put on the robe and tied the belt. "*I* ain't your friend," she said—"I ain't nobody's friend."

Quivering, he blurted the words—"Bea puts on shows here, doesn't she? . . . I know it. *Doesn't* she?"

"Well, how'd you guess it?" Darlene gave a deriding laugh. "You damn right she does!" She seemed almost to exult. "And how! You guessed it, brother. Name it and we do it—everything goes." She spoke boldly, as if to make the information more impressive, formidable—as if, really, to frighten him further. Now she sat down at her dressing table, lit a cigarette, and sleepily viewed herself in the mirror. "I told you already you better get outa here," she said. "You can see why Bea's got you here, can't you? You're *it,* man."

He stood behind her, watching her face in the mirror. Finally, he dropped his head and said nothing.

The room was small, cluttered, and crammed with personal effects. There was a television in the corner, stacks of TV and movie magazines on the dressing table, and dozens of snapshots stuck around in the edges of the mirror. The clothes closet behind her was packed tight with cheap clothes. She picked up a big comb now, but soon dropped it drunkenly on the floor. When he retrieved it for her, she grinned, then smirked, at him in the mirror.

"You better listen to what I'm tellin' you," she said. "This is a bad place—*bad*. Bea would kill me for warnin' you before she gets you set up like she wants. But I don't give a damn. Do I?—you can see I don't. That's a bunch of crap she's handin' you about getting you picked up by the police so quick. She'd put 'em on you, all right—sure, she'd do that, and wouldn't have to tell 'em who she is, either. But you could be clear outa town by the time she even found out you was gone. Suppose you sneaked outa here right now, tonight—I got keys, y'know—why, she wouldn't find out about it 'til noon, probably. Hell, you don't have to stay here. Ha—unless you want to."

There was an almost tearful grimace on his face—"But where would I go? . . . God! The police *would* pick me up! You can see that!"

"That's your problem. It's better'n staying here, though, ain't it?—especially since you know now what kinda place this is. Lord, I don't dig a guy like you—ha, and you in religious work. And another thing—a big thing—you gotta watch out for is Bertie Kalandyk. You better leave this house before you get all mixed up with him—I'm tellin' you."

"Yes, yes! . . . who is this Kalandyk?"

"He's the white fella—a real hood—that Bea runs the place for. We put on three shows a week here. Bea's got a regular troupe. White people come out here all the time to see us—two nights on the weekend and a night in the middle of the week maybe. Hell, she's talkin' about fingerin' you to the police but you could get picked up right here—in a raid. Kalandyk pays off the police captain of this dictrict, but the central vice squad—we call it the 'flying squad'—operates from outa downtown. Even Kalandyk can't do nothin' about *it,* because it roams all over town and can hit anywhere. They could knock us over any night, and then what? Why, you'd get picked up too. But anyhow you *sure* don't wanta stay around here and get involved with Kalandyk. You heard what Bea said at dinner about Chester—he was Donald's sissy partner in the show. We don't know what happened to him—probably never will. Poor Chester—everybody was crazy about him. Especially Iris. But he got in dutch with Kalandyk some way—and just disappeared. Kalandyk is one of the meanest, cruelest hoodlums and gangsters that ever lived. He's been chased outa most of the real big cities, like St. Louis and Chicago—and has ended up here. Now he's the Syndicate's man out here in the ghetto and runs everything—I mean everything. But Bea's the one that put the idea of the shows in his head—wouldn't she?—and the whole deal's turned out to be a gold mine. He's cleanin' up—the bastard. Why, every damn cop in this district out here knows about this place. Ha!—they call it 'The Hippodrome'."

Yeager took a deep breath, backed away, and sat down in the chair behind her, as she touched the big comb to her natural. Again his face was in distress—"What'll I *do?*" he said, squirming about. "Why in the world would she ever think I could be part of anything like this? . . . It's terrible!"

"Bea's crazy—*and* evil. Yeah, both. She'll try anything once. Ever since Chester disappeared, the customers have been on her to get somebody else. So has Kalandyk— although he might be the very one that knows what happened to poor Chester. So you can see why you're here, and you better listen to me and get outa here fast as you can—before it's too late."

Yeager suddenly glowered. "You're here—why haven't *you* left?"

"We wasn't talkin' about me, baby," Darlene laughed crazily. "I live the life I love, and love the life I live." She began snapping her fingers in time to imagined hot jazz.

"That's a lie," he said.

She threw down the comb and spun around. "Listen, don't you come in my room callin' *me* a liar! . . . who'n the hell d'you think you are? The reason I want you to clear outa here is because I'm thinkin' about this house —and myself! The police are swarmin' all over this town lookin' for you for knifing that big white man to death, and you could draw heat to *us.* I don't know what Bea was thinkin' about, bringin' you here. She's nuts! If the others here knew who you was, they'd lift the roof off this place—Mack Thomas would simonize you! But what you're really gonna do is hang around here 'til Bea herself gets scared and tells Kalandyk. Then you'd wish you'd been born dead, because you wouldn't live to see breakfast after he found out—as hot as you are, and drawin' heat to his place. You'd wind up in the trunk of some car with your hands and feet tied up behind you—the only way they'd ever find you is by the stink." She nodded toward the door. "Now, let me get some sleep."

After he returned to his room he made a weak attempt to pray. But it was no use—he could not. At last he undressed and went to bed.

Chapter 5

H E did not awake next morning—Friday—until after
nine o'clock, for he had not been able to sleep until
almost five. Then the awareness of his predicament—his
indecision—returned to arouse him in earnest, and he sat
up in bed, kneading his forehead and rubbing his eyes, as
if to clear his mind for some kind of action, he did not
know what. He now knew *all*—or certainly all he needed
to know. Then what was he waiting for? he thought.
Could he possibly consider staying? He hesitated, and the
glaring fact of his doubt made him abhor himself. Soon,
as respite from his thoughts, he went in the bathroom and
shaved.

Later he went to the kitchen for breakfast. He found
only Cleo and old Jessie there. Cleo was finishing the
breakfast Jessie had served her.

". . . Good morning," he said, diffidently.

Neither responded, but Cleo gave him a derisive grin.

". . . I guess I'm late," he said, his voice still timorous.

Jessie was abrupt. "There's pancakes and sausage this
mornin'. Set down at the table there. Bea left word she
wants to see you in her room when you get through eatin'."

He stopped. His throat constricted and a flaccid look

63

came on his face. "Bea . . . yes. Which is her room?" he finally said, and sat down.

"Way up the hall—second room from the front, on the left-hand side." Jessie then limped over to the stove and brought him back a cup of coffee. He took it with trembling hands.

When Cleo had finished her breakfast she sat smoking a cigarette. Soon she was coughing. Jessie glared at the cigarette, then at her—"Nobody kaint tell you anything," Jessie said. "You still keep puffin' one of them dadblasted coffin nails right aftah another. You're commitin' suicide, that's whut you're doin'." Cleo grinned, shrugged, and continued smoking.

When Jessie brought Yeager's pancakes and sausage, Cleo laughed—"That's right, Jessie. Fatten him up good. Donald's been on cloud nine ever since Willie got here— he's forgot all about Chester already, ha! But Willie'll never be a Chester, you can tell that—you can bet on it. Wasn't Chester somethin'?—with his long silver fingernails and shantung suits. Oh, God, was he a scream! Everybody loved Chester—Iris most of all, because he spent so much time with her and read her the comic books. And, Lord, the customers!—Oh, was that boy a crowd-pleaser! Wow! Willie could never make a Chester if he tried a hundred years—everybody at the table last night could see that. Ha!—except Donald."

Jessie raised her eyes sanctimoniously to the ceiling—
"Lord Gawd, this Sodom and Gomorrah!" She poured
them both more coffee.

Cleo, on reflection, laughed grimly—"Yet, y'can't tell.
Willie just might learn the ropes. It's possible, I guess.
Huh, Jessie?"

Jessie gave a theatrical sigh—"Unless Gawd A'mighty
strikes him down with a bolt of lightnin' first."

Bea's summons had rendered the food in Yeager's
mouth tasteless. He ate one pancake and a small piece of
the sausage and pushed his plate away. Soon he got up and,
dour, saying no more to the women, returned to his room.
He stood by the dresser, in fear—confused, inept, yet in
deep concentration. How should she be confronted? he
asked himself. But need she be confronted at all?—if he
had really decided to leave. Had he, though? he thought
—that was the question. Nevertheless, he finally left his
room and went up the hall. When he knocked on her door,
her heavy voice came through at once—"Come on in!"

He opened the door into what looked like a hotel room.
It was large, with wall-to-wall carpeting, and furnished
in a mélée of gauche, calamitous colors. Also, there was
an air conditioner, now winter-covered, in one window
and the big color television Bismarck had mentioned in
front of the window adjacent. Bea was seated in an arm-
chair, in lounging pajamas and gold lamé house slippers,

and, having just buffed her nails, was using a purse mirror in tweezering her eyebrows—all as she half-watched an early TV quiz show. And for some unknown reason she wore her huge red wig this morning—her hostess wig— its flowing Nordic tresses falling almost to her shoulders. Was it the gravity, the crisis, of the occasion? he wondered. "Close the door," she said, eyeing him intently—"Iris was tellin' me you was sick last night."

". . . I feel okay now." His voice was dry and thin and he seldom looked at her.

She waved her lacquered nails toward a chair. "Set down," she said—"Y'know one thing, I don't like your attitude too much. Instead of goin' around here with a long face on all the time, you oughta be tryin' to make friends with the people here in the house. It's for your own good, y'know. But the way you're actin' is no damn good for yourself or for me, either. It makes 'em suspicious of you. Wise up. Can't you smile, or laugh, once in awhile? . . . or do a little talkin' sometimes?—God!"

He had sat down, but now gave her only a doleful look. He said nothing.

"Well anyhow," she told him, "I sent for you because I wanta talk to you. It's important—serious." She got up and turned off the television and his heart rate quickened. "The reason I want you to start snappin' out of it is because we're in the entertainment business here. It's simple—we're entertainers. We can't go mopin' around like you been doin' ever since you been here and expect people to like us. People just won't take to us—and we won't like each other much, either. We're meetin' the public all the time and have got to do a lot of grinnin' and carryin' on whether we like it or not. And we got to get along with each other too—if we don't it'll show up in *our* business in a minute."

He was breathing so deeply he could only look at her.

"Did you see that big room up there?" she said, pointing toward the front—"the one off the foyer? Well, we give shows up there." She paused a moment to watch him. "They ain't no cabaret shows, either," she said. "They're stronger stuff than that. Let's see . . ."—she began counting on her fingers—"there's Mavis. Cleo. And Darlene . . . that's the girls. And Mack Thomas. Donald. And . . . well, Chester . . . he ain't with us no more. That's five, ain't it? —yes. Well, they're the ones that do the shows. They're all right, too—I may have to give 'em hell once in awhile, but they ain't a bad bunch most of the time. They all get along good together, too—there ain't nothin' more important than that. That's why I want you to get more friendly with 'em—get in with 'em. Take tonight, for instance. There'll be another mob here, just like there was night before last—only, this time, you'll get to see 'em, because I want you to help out Bismarck on the bar. Just tonight, though. But it'll give you a chance to kinda get the hang of the place . . . to see how we operate, and just what goes on."

Yeager had a stricken look on his face. At last he looked at her. "My cigarettes are all gone," he said weakly— "could I have one of yours?"

She reached for her pack and gave him a cigarette. "There's a carton or two in the cupboard in the kitchen," she said. "Pick up a couple packs when you go back there." She also took a cigarette. When she lit his, she saw his trembling hand. "What you shaking about?" she said.

He dragged hungrily on the cigarette but would not look at her now.

"I was gonna tell you a little bit about my boys and girls here," she said. "Take Cleo, for instance. She's sick. I don't know how sick, because she won't go to a doctor. I'm worried about her, though. She's a good girl at heart, but has had a rough time, an awful rough time. She was married at one time to a damn sax player and had two nice kids before things started goin' wrong. But this cat was runnin' around on her and treatin' her bad to boot— fightin' her. This went on for a couple of years. Then she started drinkin', tryin' to keep what he was doin' off her mind. And that was her downfall—things went from bad to worse. Before long they had split up and the judge gave the kids to his mother. Yeah, his mother—it damn near killed Cleo. She'll never get over it as long as she lives. Then she really started goin' down—'til I practically took her off the street. Yeah, I rescued her, in a way. You can see what a beauty she was at one time, but now she's got kinda hardened and coarse in her ways—rough-actin'. If it hadn't been for me, though, there's no tellin' what'd happened to her by now."

Yeager stared at her and swallowed.

"And there's Mack Thomas," she said. "He started out as a two-bit fighter. He was a pimp, too, for awhile . . . then a tinhorn gambler, and finally just any kinda hustler—'til he come with me. I've about got him on his feet now. But Mack don't give a damn about nothin' but food and women—that's all. And that's all he'll ever give a second thought to the rest of his life. He's probably the favorite one of all of 'em with the customers . . . well, either him or Mavis. The peckerwoods think he's terrific. Wouldn't they? But he *is*. He's a sight to see in action, I'll tell you —a regular stud horse. Bert Kalandyk pays him good, too —but Bertie pays 'em all good. So Mack's got it made— he's doin' what he likes more'n anything in the world to do and gettin' paid for it. He's gotta leadpipe cinch. So what's he do? Why, he gets a touch of the big-head every once in awhile—and if Bertie wasn't in the picture, Mack might get kinda hard to handle. But he's as scared of Bertie Kalandyk as the devil is of holy water. It shows he's got *some* sense, I guess."

Yeager accepted another cigarette and sat on the edge of his chair inhaling deeply.

"Mavis is a South Carolina geechie," Bea said—"from one of them old tidewater rice plantations. She's been away from there since she was seventeen, but she's only been with me about five months. Ain't she the prettiest little thing you ever laid your eyes on? Lord have mercy, is she fine! She come from a family of fourteen kids— think of that. She's crazy about old Bismarck for some reason or other—looks up to him sorta like he was her father. Maybe it's because she can't go home no more and misses her own folks—I don't know. Anyhow, her and old Bismarck are real tight buddies. He spends a lotta time with her, tellin' her all about his many different experi- ences in life—and old Bismarck's had 'em, too, believe me. And he kids around with her a lot—ha, tells her one of these days, if she ain't careful, she's goin' to come up with a watermelon under her apron. And all that kinda stuff. They're a pair."

"How long has Darlene been with you?" Yeager said, fidgeting, unable to control his grimace.

Bea promptly, angrily, waved him off—"Don't bring up that Darlene! I have more trouble with her than all the rest of 'em put together—especially lately. She's got a bad case of the big-head now, too, y'know—maybe I oughta say 'hard-head.' But that ain't the way it was when I first brought her here—no indeed. She was humble as pie then. The first time I ever saw her was in a tavern. She was runnin' with some of the rattiest niggers you ever saw in your life. There ain't no way of knowin' where she'd be today if I hadn't picked her up—maybe dead. I remind her about it, too, every time she gets up on her high horses like she does sometimes. And she can be stubborn as hell. She forgets damn quick all I've done for her. It burns me up, too. Yeah, she was hustlin' the taverns when I first run into her—she'll still turn a trick every once in awhile if you don't watch her like a hawk. You shoulda seen her about a year ago when I first brought her here. She was dirty and broke and raggedy as a jaybird. And half sick on top of that . . . A little while before that she'd tried—*herself,* mind you—to get rid of a baby. It damn near killed her. She almost bled to death. When I first come across her, she was still tryin' to get her strength back. Yet was hustlin' right on—she had to eat. But *now* look at her. She's got her health back, got a closet full of shoes and coats and dresses back there, and a habit of sassin' me whenever she feels like it. I gotta few drinks in me one night and whipped her ass all over this house. She'll never forget it, I bet. But Darlene's no fool altogether. She's got an awful keen mind in some things—can be cagey as hell. At heart she don't like me, though—I know it, y'see. *You* better watch her, too. Remember, she knows your secret—always remember that."

Yeager spun around in his chair and stared out the window, as if he could bear hearing no more.

But soon Bea's eyes began darting back and forth. She was thinking fast. Then a cunning look came on her face. ". . . Let's see," she said—"Who does that leave . . .? Have we missed anybody? Oh, of course—Donald! Yeah—now, *there's* one for the books. Well, he's a faggot, of course. You could tell that—you'd have to be deaf, dumb, and blind to miss that. But get this, he's one of the nicest fellas you'll ever wanta meet. He'll give anybody the shirt right offa his back. He's been with me from the very beginnin' —through thick and thin—and if I gotta pet around here other'n Iris, it's Donald, I'll tell you that. He never knowed who his parents was, y'know—he just growed up. But he went to high school some way. Of course, he can't help the way he was born, his sex. Nature just played a trick on him, that's all. Well anyhow, *he's* the one you wanta get to know, because you'll be spendin' a lotta time with him. Treat him right and he'll treat you right—and I'll treat you right, too. But don't kid yourself—I ain't playin'. This is a deadly serious business—if you knowed Bert Kalandyk, you'd know how serious it is. And get this straight—I ain't hurt in the least about your feelin's. I couldn't care less. What the hell, I brought you in here off the street, didn't I? If it wasn't for me, you'd already been before the grand jury by now. You're God-damn lucky—so *I* ain't sheddin' any crocodile tears over you. Like I told you before, what happens to you from here on in is strictly up to you. You ain't got but two ways to go —my way or the police's. It's just that simple. I went to the trouble of explainin' all this to you simply for your own good. And you'll be damn wise to take it that way, too."

Yeager was grimacing wildly now, yet sat erect in the chair with his arms rigid at his side, as if struggling to control himself. But finally a desperate, tearful look came on his face as he turned to her again. Yet he could not speak.

Bea stood up now. "Okay," she said, "that's all for right now. Be ready to help out Bismarck on the bar tonight, though." Then she went to her closet and took down a shopping bag. "Here," she said, handing it to him, "put them bloody clothes of yours in here and bring it back, so I can take 'em downstairs to the furnace and burn 'em."

Yeager took the bag with him and returned to his room.

Chapter 6

THAT evening, as it was getting dark, Bismarck brought a white jacket to Yeager's room. In the gloaming of the unlighted room and from the bed on which he sat, Yeager, seeming stuporous, peered up at the old man as if he had never seen him before. Bismarck dropped the jacket on the bed. "Did'ja ever tend bar before?" he asked in his peevish voice, moving his dentures around. Yeager's upturned face now had a bewildered, dazzled look—he seemed not to hear. "Ain't you goin' to eat dinner?" Bismarck said. "You'll need it, 'cause we gotta hard night ahead of us."

Yeager was submissive. ". . . I'll eat," he said.

"On show nights we eat in the kitchen," Bismarck explained. "There ain't much time, so Jessie feeds us there —first come, first served. I can almost tell you ain't never tended bar before—ain't that right?"

Yeager got up and, eyes half closed, groping, put on the light—but still seemed deaf.

"I figured you hadn't," Bismarck said testily. "You ain't gonna be much help, I can see that. But it's another one of Bea's brain storms. Okay, I'll fix the cocktails, then —the martinis and Manhattans—and you can take care of the beer, and some of the highballs, maybe. I bet you don't even know how to fix a Scotch and soda."

Yeager was oblivious. He stood looking at Bismarck. "Have you got a Bible in your room you could let me have for awhile?" he said. ". . . or the New Testament?"

Bismarck stared at him. "You asked me that before. No, I ain't got a Bible any more. I read the catechism. Darlene's the only one around here with a Bible, I think —or Jessie, maybe." He went to the door to go. "After you eat," he said, "you'kin help me take some of the stuff up front and get the bar set up." He left.

At last Yeager was conscious of his hunger. Yet he resisted going to the kitchen for another half-hour. When finally he went, he ate a hurried, nervous dinner of Jessie's meatballs and spaghetti and returned to his room. He stood at his window again looking out into the darkness—the weather had worsened and the night was wet and raw. Soon he sat down and tried to watch television, but at once dreading the prospect of seeing a newscast, he quickly turned it off—he wanted nothing from the outside world, and somehow knew now this fact was the very crux of his dilemma.

Before long he could hear the apartment beginning to come alive, and recognized what it meant—already his watch showed 7:30 and, remembering his first night in the house and what Bea had told him today, he understood these preparatory sounds. Far up front the little phonograph was going again, and from all the rooms along the hall came the noise of the troupe's coarse highjinks. He could hear Cleo's raucous voice and in another room, a laughing squeal from Donald; later Mack Thomas yelled an obscenity up the hall at giggling Mavis. But Darlene's room was quiet.

Finally at 7:50 Bismarck came. "Let's go," he said, irritably. "Git your white coat. Everything's ready—the bar's all set up. I done it all myself."

Yeager put on the white jacket and followed him up the hall. The huge foyer was ablaze with lights now. And the little bar was well-stocked and ready for business, as Bismarck poured himself a rewarding creme de menthe. But the double doors to the arena were still closed.

"As soon as they start comin'," Bismarck instructed, "fill some of them highball glasses with ice cubes—it'll save time when they get to pressin' us. And 'til we get real busy, you can take the people's coats and hang 'em on the long rack there. Now while we got a minute or two put some more ice in that tub of beer—cover the bottles good." Then Bismarck, immaculate in his white jacket as he leaned against the bar, sipped the liqueur and viewed Yeager with disdainful curiosity.

At 8:15 the doorbell rang for the first time.

"Here we go," Bismarck said, and came out quickly

from behind the bar. He went over and pushed the buzzer, unlocked the three locks, and opened the door. At once they heard a thunder of feet ascending the three flights of stairs. Yeager's heartbeat seemed to treble.

Now, Bea, in another of her glittering, low-cut dresses, her huge red wig in place, rushed out of her room and up the hall to greet the guests. As she passed through the foyer she glanced at Yeager, and lost her temper—"Goddamn it to hell, can you *smile?* . . . For just once in your life, *smile,* will 'ya!" In the next instant she was at the door herself flashing a mechanically brilliant smile at the three young white men Bismarck had just admitted.

The men looked like truck drivers. And one seemed slightly drunk already. He was lean and hatless with a dark lock of hair down over one eye. His two stocky companions looked enough alike to be twins.

"Hi, Bea," the lean fellow grinned. "How'ya doin'?"

"Hi, boys," Bea laughed. "What?—only three of youse? Sounded like a herd of buffaloes comin' up the stairs. I thought maybe you was bringin' me a bunch of nice new customers. Come on in."

"We ain't got any millionaire friends, Bea," one of the stocky twins laughed—"I know they're what you're lookin' for." The men gave their coats to waiting, still unsmiling, Yeager, who took them over to the rack. The same twin rubbed his cold hands together. "That damn rain's turned into sleet and snow out there," he said, and looked eagerly over toward the bar—"Hey, I want summa that 100-proof bourbon, Bea. But is it still a dollar a drink?" He laughed again.

Bea touched her red wig and attempted a kittenish smile. "Why, sure, sweetheart," she said. "It's either Jack Daniels or Old Fitzgerald Bonded, y'know—I don't handle no rot-gut whiskey. But you-all ain't reached that stage yet —you ain't by the gate yet, boys."

The other twin grinned, then began fumbling in his pants pocket and pulled out a money clip. "For ten bucks apiece," he said, "you oughta throw in Mavis, Bea."

"Oh, that Mavis!" the lean, tipsy fellow crooned, closing his eyes in ecstasy. "Bea, Bea!—when you gonna introduce me to her?"

Bea was busy taking the two twenty-dollar bills handed her by the twin with the money clip. When she had given him back ten dollars change, she turned and answered the question—"I keep tellin' you, sugar, this ain't no cat house. This is a *thee-ater*—Mavis is an actress. I can't seem to get that through your head." She gave a booming laugh and stuck the two twenties in a business-size brown envelope she carried in her hand. The men laughed and shook their heads as they went over to the bar.

"Hi, oldtimer," the first twin said to Bismarck.

"Why, good evenin'." Bismarck gave them all a quick,

false smile. "What can we do for you fellas this evenin'?"

The lean tipsy one got out his wallet now. "I'm buyin'," he said to the others. "If Wally can put thirty bucks in this deal, I can spend three. Three Jack Daniels' and water," he said to Bismarck.

Suddenly Yeager was startled by the jarring noise of the doorbell again. Bea was manning the door now. She pushed the buzzer, opened the door, and waited. When she saw the two new arrivals round the top bend in the stairs, her face went into a frenzy of unctuous smiles. "Ooooooh, my! . . . Good evenin', good evenin', Mr. Hampstill! Good evenin', Miss Smith!" She beamed and fawned as she admitted a distinguished-looking man in his late fifties, who escorted a young lady about twenty-eight. The lady was attractive despite a narcotized, droop-eyed expression that made her appear drowsy or half asleep. Both were elegantly dressed—she in some French couturier's original, a suit, with her dark hair parted prissily in the middle and a ball in the back. The man's hair was reddish brown, mixed with grey at the temples—his complexion very ruddy. "Oh, come right in!" Bea exulted. The man smiled whimsically and put out his hand, which Bea shook gratefully. He then took a thin booklike wallet from his jacket's inside pocket and fingered out of it a brand new bill, which he handed to Bea, then raised his palm to indicate he desired no change. Bea jumped,

bucked her eyes, squealed, and laughed sychophantly—
"Oh, oh, Mr. Hampstill! You're always so sweet I could
kiss you!! Instead I'll kiss this beautiful century note!"
She put the crisp one hundred-dollar bill to her big lips
and kissed it hungrily, then let out another little screech
of delight.

Yeager stood dourly behind her to take the couple's
wraps. But Bea took them herself and barked an order at
him. *"Willie,* go back there in the kitchen right quick—
hurry up, now!—and get one of them bottles of champagne out of the refrigerator and bring two champagne
glasses with it. I want Mr. Hampstill and Miss Smith
here to have all the champagne they want. *Hurry up,*
now!" Yeager left quickly, and Bea hurried back into her
bedroom with the two coats. The couple had moved over
against the far foyer wall now and stood to themselves,
looking awkward, lost, as they glanced uncomfortably at
the three loud truck drivers at the bar. But soon Miss
Smith's eyes were half closed again, almost as if she were
on some cool, psychedelic trip; she seemed interested in
nothing—had watched Bea's performance sleepily, cynically, smiling only once. On the surface Mr. Hampstill
appeared at ease, yet seemed suffering some suppressed,
pathological excitement; his face was flushed, his eyes
enkindled. Soon Yeager returned with the iced champagne
and glasses, and when, struggling, he finally popped the

cork, the truck drivers spun around gaping. At last the twin Wally grinned. "How much is *that* a drink, Bea?" he called over. Again Bea vainly touched her wig—"Ah, you'd never, never, guess, boys."

Two couples arrived next. But they were one party— all men. The first pair entering were tall youths, fair and languorous-looking—one with long, blond hair, the other a mademoiselle's sweet smile. Their two friends behind them were somewhat more disparate, and even more bizarre. One, svelte, young, wearing a tightly-belted trench coat, was Latin-dark, with large, staring, truculent eyes. But his companion was near sixty, and blubbery fat; he wore a balloonlike trench coat, a beret, and was smoking a cheroot. Yeager, although now busy behind the bar, stared at them. The fat man seemed the only one who knew Bea. "I've brought along three friends," he said to her in a soft, matronly voice, laughing as he paid her— "Do I get a commission?" Bea was busy fitting the four tens into her brown envelope. "You deserve one, at that, Mr. Sweeny, honey, if only I could afford it!" she guffawed at last, then looked at the three youths with him—"Say, you're travelin' in some awful good-lookin' company to-night. . . . Ain't you gettin' pretty foxy, now, for a man your age? Ha! ha! ha!—My! Be young to stay young, eh? Well, there ain't nothin' wrong with that—nothin' at all." Sweeny was pleased with these blandishments and, smiling proudly, introduced his friends—"This is Darin, Bea," he said of one of the tall, fair youths. "And Harold." Then he turned around to the fiery-eyed Latin, and hesitated—mooning. "Bea, this is Miguel," he said possessively, plaintively. Sleek-looking, dark Miguel gave Bea a haughty glance and nodded, but did not smile. Yeager now stood waiting and took all their coats. Soon they went over to the bar, where Sweeny bought the drinks.

Two women and a man made up the next party to arrive. They were well dressed, but in a flashy, theatrical way, and all were sun-lamped a deep berry brown, though their hands were milk white. Both women were at least in their middle fifties, but by their thigh-length dresses and selected hair hues, they seemed straining to appear in their twenties. The man was thick-set and squat, with the blunt nose and high cheekbones of a Slav. On the third finger of his right hand he wore a heavy square-set ring that was often in view, for he constantly picked his nose. Bea was friendly, but not effusive, as she greeted them and took their money. "It's nice to see you-all agin," she said. "Bea," the hawk-eyed woman with the raven hair said, "you haven't forgotten what we suggested to you last time, have you?" Bea looked uneasy—"No, I ain't forgot, Mrs. Chance. But that ain't easy, y'know." Then the second woman, the hard-eyed silver blond, spoke up—"You want to have something for *all* your guests, don't you, Bea? . . .

not just for some of them. You need some younger people
—we've told you that." Bea went stony-faced, cool. "I
don't think you kin get any," she said; "You kaint even
get any teen-agers, much less what you-all want—children." The man withdrew his finger from his nose and
said impatiently—"Well, have you *tried?*" Bea smiled
coldly—"No, to tell you the truth, Mr. Nikone, I ain't.
I kinda draw the line on kids." Soon the trio, sighing
futilely, gave their coats to Yeager, withdrew, and went
over to the bar.

The doorbell rang again. When Bea opened the door,
the lone newcomer, on the run, was already rounding the
top bend in the stairs. The moment she saw him she gave
an annoyed snort of frustration. He was a red-faced, un-
kempt, shabby man of fifty, with a wild shock of yellow
hair that his hat could not entirely conceal. Yet he carried
a briefcase—and in the other hand, a plastic-wrapped side
of bacon. He came in laughing, and held up the bacon in
triumph. "Look!" he whispered excitedly—"Look, sweetheart! I brought you something. Take it. It's for you—no
foolin'!" He thrust the bacon at her. She sighed, but finally
smiled once and took it. Then she shook her head in
warning: "Now, Marty—it takes more'n a piece of bacon
to get in here, y'know." Ignoring her warning, he tried
flattery: "Oh, your wig! ... er, I mean your hair—it's a
real beaut, baby. Golleee!" Then he showed a five-dollar

bill he had held concealed in his hand and stepped closer, whispering again: "Look, Bea, sweetie, I'm a little short tonight—I ain't got ten bucks on me. You go on and take this fiver, and I'll make it up next time around, see?" Bea pursed her lips and turned her head away—"Oh, no, you don't, Marty. I told you last time—no more credit. You gotta go, now. I'm sorry, but I can't run a business this way." She tried to return the bacon. "No, no, that's yours," he said, refusing it, and laughed again—"Then, how about letting me come in just long enough to buy myself a drink, and then get goin'?" "No," she said, "if I let you in, you won't wanta leave. Come on, now, Marty, let's go." She called Yeager over and gave him the bacon. Soon Marty's face lit up again. "*I* know!" he said to her —"Just let me see *half* the show for the five bucks . . . or even just Mavis's and Mack's act. Yeah, I'll sure settle for them two any time. Whew!—any time, any place, anywhere! How 'bout it, sweetheart?—come on." He tried to make her take the five-dollar bill. *"No!"* she said flatly—"No, I won't! Now, I ain't got time, here on one of my busiest nights, to stand here and jaw with you no longer." The doorbell rang. "Y'see?—you're holdin' me up, Marty!" She went and pushed the buzzer, then took him by the elbow—"All right, let's go. Come on back some other night. You gotta go, now." She opened the door. "Okay, okay, sweetheart," he laughed—"I'll get

lost, if that's what you want. No hard feelings." He left
and ran back down the stairs.

Halfway down, he passed a troop of other patrons
coming up. When they reached the top, there were
three G. I.'s in uniform and six or seven conventioneers,
all convoyed by T-Bone Sims, one of Bea's brokers, who
lived with his big family in the apartment below. They
had hardly entered when the doorbell rang again. It
seemed all the guests were arriving at once now, the stairs
creaking under their weight. Soon Bea's brown envelope
was bulging and the foyer resembled a weird, tumultuous
cocktail party. Bismarck and Yeager perspired freely trying
to keep up with the clamor for drinks. The double doors
to the arena were still closed, but all eyes played desperately, if furtively, on them, as the patrons continued
to come. The foyer was soon packed, and further milling
around with a drink in hand was almost impossible. Now
there was only the deep, excited hubbub of voices that
Yeager had heard on that first night. Although busy
behind the bar, he glanced over at Bea at the door—
in the press of the commotion her wig was askew now
and a red ringlet had fallen down over one eye. But he
knew the cocktail hour would soon be over and fear
clutched his heart.

Still another guest was arriving—an old fat woman
had just slowly panted up the three flights of stairs. Flesh

flabby, eyes rheumy, her blue-white cheeks nevertheless were severely rouged—as she still gasped for breath coming in the door. Bea greeted her with mock exaggerated joy. "Now I *know* my night's a success!—Mrs. Wade's here!" she cried, rushing to the old woman, who, though breathless, finally answered her in a petulant Southern accent: "Jesus Redeemah! . . . whew!—Bea, ah've climbed them damn stairs fuh the last time! That ah guarantee you! When you put an elevatah in this place, ah'll be back—and not a night befoh!" "Oh, Mrs. Wade, where would I ever git that kinda money?" Bea simpered, ". . . and in somebody else's buildin'. Don't be so hard on me!" The old woman had her admission money wadded up in her fist, and now pressed it into Bea's hand. "Mrs. Wade, you know we couldn't git along without you—you know that," Bea said, stealthily unwadding the bill to verify its denomination before she worked it into her swollen brown envelope. The old woman came close now, put her arm partway around Bea's girth, and laughed in her face; then whispered—"If you evah git rid of that Mack Thomas, you'll *sho* nevah see me agin. He-he-he-he!" Bea bucked the whites of her eyes, guffawed, and whispered back in the old woman's ear—"Why, Mrs. Wade, I knowed that's whut was bringin' you here all the time. *Haw!*" Both laughing convulsively, they fell into each other's arms.

Meanwhile, little Iris had entered the foyer. Now she somehow surfaced out of the frantic, jostling crowd, coming up near the bar. She was selling cigarettes, and had an opened carton in her hand and one unopened under her arm. Yeager stared in astonishment, but Bismarck, laughing, called to her—"Iris! Hey, Iris! Wanta drink? Come over here and I'll give'ya a drink...ha, a drink'a ginger ale, that is. Come on, sweetheart!" Iris twisted and fought her way through to the bar, then stopped and studied Bismarck for a moment. Finally she grinned at him—"I'm too busy. I ain't got no time for a drink." Then soon she was swallowed up in the crowd again.

In all of the noise it had now become so difficult to hear the jarring doorbell that Bea left the door open and went and stood directly under the bell. The next time it sounded, she merely pressed the buzzer. Someone came bounding up the stairs, and soon bedraggled Marty reappeared in the doorway—his straw hair shooting wildly from under his hat. He still carried the briefcase—and this time a ten-dollar bill, which he immediately brandished under Bea's nose. "Stand back, sweetheart!" he crowed—"I got money!" "Oh, God," Bea sighed. She took the money and let him pass. But suddenly her face clouded up and she called him back. "Now, listen," she warned, "I don't wanta hear a peep outa you in there tonight." She pointed to the still-closed arena. "Everybody else is always quiet, Marty. But, oh no, not *you*—you gotta keep up a runnin' talk all the time, commentin' on everything, egging 'em on. Remember, you ain't at a baseball game, yellin' every time somebody hits a home-run. It's vulgar! The other people around you don't like it a bit. They want everything quiet, real quiet. They ain't just lookin', y'know—they're listenin', too. It's gotta be *quiet*." Marty, though in a hurry and inattentive, laughed—"Okay, just as you say, sweetheart! Ain't you the boss?"

He lunged his way through to the bar, emerging in front of Yeager. "How'ya doin', boy?" he said. Yeager glared at him before he thought. Marty said—"All I want is a half a glass of Seven Up. How much'll that cost me?" Though busy, sweating, Bismarck heard the familiar voice, and spoke up—"Our Seven Up is a mixer for our drinks. We sell whiskey. If you still want some Seven Up, you'kin have it, but it'll cost'ya a dollar like every-thing else." Marty, unfazed, laughed bitterly—"Okay, Uncle Bismarck, you got the whip hand tonight. Gimme a gin and Seven Up, then." He put a dollar bill on the bar. Yeager mixed and handed him the highball and took the money. Marty promptly drank off half the drink, took a pint of gin out of his briefcase, filled the glass back up to the top, and stirred it with his grimy finger.

Hate in his eyes, he raised the glass and saluted Bismarck
—"*This* won't cost me nothin', will it, uncle?" Then he
turned and was lost in the crowd. "That . . . that hyena!"
Bismarck spluttered.

Suddenly they heard a shrill, tipsy outcry from some
woman in the crowd—"*Atta gal, Bea!*" Then a man
shouted hoarsely—"Here we go, boys! . . . Here we go!"
Another man jumped up on a chair and Yeager saw that
it was straw-haired Marty again, wildly waving his
drink and bellowing repeatedly—"All ashore that's goin'
ashore!" The veins stood out in Marty's neck and temples
as he tried to be heard above all the clamor. Finally,
Yeager saw Bea. She was laughing and flourishing a bunch
of keys high over her head for everyone to see, as she
shouldered her way through the mélée over toward the
big double doors to the arena. Yeager grew faint from
fear. The crowd surged close behind her. When at last
she reached the doors, she quickly unlocked them—and
swung them wide. The crowd cheered. Now she flicked
on the solitary light dangling far over in the center of
the room above the cot. When she finally stepped aside,
the procession, like excited cattle, began pushing and
shoving its way through the doors. Yeager glanced at
his watch. It was 9:25. He was afraid even to look in
Bea's direction—fearing her slightest attention.

Meanwhile, Bea had returned to the front door to

make sure it was closed and all three locks locked. She was turning away—when once more the doorbell sounded. She stopped, and frowned—knowing the show was already late. At last she started over to the buzzer. But stopped again. Next came a long, impatient ring. She finally went over and pressed the buzzer, then returned and unlocked the three locks again. As she stood in the door waiting, the sounds of at least two pairs of heavy feet echoed up the stairwell. Then suddenly, hearing familiar men's voices, she stiffened.

Soon, approaching the top landing, two black men appeared. On impulse she make a quick motion to slam the door in their faces. But she held her outrage and instead gave a bitter, persecuted sigh. "You're too late, boys," she said, and blocked the door. They ignored her and continued their climb up to the doorway. The chunky fellow in front, a knife scar from his temple to his jaw, grinned drunkenly and looked past her at three stragglers still in the foyer. "You ain't started yet," he said—"so how 'kin we be late?" They confronted her on the threshold. The second man, who was tall and surly, peered over the shoulder of the first. Bea now spoke pleadingly, almost tearfully, to the grinning man in front: "Oh, hell, Barney!—why don't you-all come back some other time! . . . I gotta houseful tonight!—honest to God, I have!" Both men looked in again at the three white patrons finishing their drinks in the foyer, then at Bismarck and Yeager dismantling the bar. Barney's grin vanished. "Don't hand us that shit," he said—"You mean you gotta Jim Crow house here, and fuh us to git t'hell outa here. That's whut you mean!" They could not see to the right directly into the arena, but Barney, pointing toward it, added—"I'll bet you a hundred dollars to one there ain't a nigger in that room." He reached fumblingly in his hip pocket for his wallet—"You'kin make yourself a hundred bucks right now if there's one nigger in that place!" His voice had gotten loud and Bismarck and Yeager looked apprehensive. Bea, guilty, stood helpless.

The tall, surly fellow behind, who seemed sober, now shoved Barney through the door and followed him. "She ain't gotta Jim Crow party *now*," he said, and turned on Bea—"Yeah, you gotta houseful of paddy freaks in there and don't want no niggers. Well, you got two now. We're payin' just like they did." He turned to Barney, who had his wallet out now, and took a twenty-dollar bill from him. "Here, here's a double-sawbuck "—he tried to give Bea the money. In an incoherent rage, she knocked it out of his hand to the floor. The man bristled and his eyes got big—"Woman, whut the goddam hell's wrong with you?" he said, stooping and picking the money up—"That green'll spend just like theirs!" Meanwhile, his friend Barney had staggered over to the bar. "Don't put that whiskey away yet," he said to Bismarck. "Give us two double bourbons." The three frightened white stragglers quickly left and went into the arena.

Bea came running over to the bar now—apoplectic. "*You* know the police don't like no black and tan parties!" she railed at the interlopers. "I don't have to tell you that!— you know it! You know there ain't nothin' I can do about it, either! Then, why would you come bargin' in here tryin' to make trouble for me?—huh? You know I gotta do business with 'em. Then, why would you do it? Y'wanta know why? I'll tell you! It's because you're two motherfuckin' *niggers!* That's why!" She was waving her arms, spluttering, yelling, and choking with rage— "Oh! . . . Oh! . . . I hate a God-damn nigger!" She rushed off down the hall, but suddenly wheeled and came back— "I started to go get my pistol and kill botha you! But, no, I ain't gonna do that! I'm gonna let you go right in and enjoy the show!—go on, go right ahead! And tonight I'm gonna get on the phone and call Bertie Kalandyk— I'm gonna tell him how Barney Coleman and Railhead Struthers tried to get his place knocked over. That's all I gotta do!—and I'm gonna do it if Christ lets me live 'till this show's over tonight! When Bertie's boys get through with you with them burp-guns of theirs, you'll both be layin' out in some vacant lot lookin' like a couple of sieves! That's a promise! Put that liquor away,

Bismarck—the bar's closed!"

Barney and Railhead had gradually become statues—with faces of cautious, reflective sobriety. They studied Bea's fury and then each other. There was silence. Finally Barney tried an uncomfortably false laugh. "Jesus Christ A'mighty, Bea," he said, "we didn't know you was gonna have triplets about it. You're playin' us cheap—hell, why would we wanta hang around here any more'n you'd want us to? You ain't runnin' nothin' here but a goddam three-ring circus for a bunch of peckerwood queers, anyhow. Come on, Rail, let's git t'hell outa this dive." They both drifted toward the door now.

Bea followed them, harassing, taunting—"Oh, no! You ain't leavin', are you? . . . Why don't you stay around and see the show?—that's whut you come here for, ain't it? Whut's changed your mind so quick?—huh? No, you got plenty sense!—you God-damn right you have! Don't you never in life put your feet on them stairs agin! *Never!*" She flung the door open and stepped back. When they had barely crossed the threshold, she slammed the door with such force it brought down plaster dust.

As soon as she could lock the three locks again, she started running frantically down the hall, beating on all the doors—crying to her troupe—"Okay, okay, let's go! Show time! Show time! Oh, my God, we're late as hell already! Come on, you-all! *Come on!*" Suddenly remembering something, she spun around and yelled for Iris. Bismarck gave her a displeased look. "Where *is* that little black spasm?" she bellowed at him—"Ketch her and lock her up!"

Bismarck ground his dentures angrily. "Where d'you *think* she is!" he said. "She's hidin'!—'cause she don't wanta be locked up!"

"Bismarck, you find her and lock her up in my room! She's just like an eel—you gotta watch her every minute. *I* ain't got time to go find her!" Suddenly she stared at the open doors of the arena—"Oh, Lord, she might be somewhere in there right now."

"No, she ain't, either," Bismarck said. "I saw to that. Go on, now—I know where she is. She's in my room, and I'll be there with her."

Bea sighed and, already oblivious of Bismarck, stared with hot impatience, frustration, down the hall. "Just think," she bemoaned to him and Yeager, "I ain't only gotta go in there and apologize for the show bein' late, I gotta tell 'em I'm still a man short again—Oh, God!" Furtively, Yeager took up a tray of used glasses and started to the kitchen with them. "Don't leave, Willie," she ordered—"Stick around." He felt his throat tighten, his lower abdomen toss—he really wanted to break and run, to hide, but where? he thought. Finally, hands trembling, he put the tray back down, yet somehow stood staring at her. But now she rushed off down the hall again, once more beating on all the doors, and when Mack Thomas at last stepped from his room, she turned on him in a fury—"For Christ's sake! . . . It's about time!" She flung Mavis' door open—"Come outa there, Mavis! . . . What's *keepin'* you-all!"

Mack came up into the foyer and stood coolly waiting— squat, powerful, barefoot, brutish, clad only in a robe. He grinned slightly but was otherwise as detached as a rock.

Mavis came out of her room wearing only tiny soft house slippers and a tangerine robe. She was heavily made-up and her lips were parted in a daring smile. Yeager stared at her carnal beauty.

Now Cleo emerged—tall, gaunt, deathly pale, in a short white robe. She too was composed, even ice-like. Besides the myriad rings on her bony fingers, she wore unusual earrings which were strangely old-fashioned and delicate, as if heirlooms.

At last, down at the end of the hall, Darlene came out of her room—wearing a violet-flowered kimono. Yeager's eyes followed her as she came toward them. Halfway up the hall she met Donald coming out, and they came the rest of the way together. Yeager glanced at Bea and, wondering what was next for him, stiffened with fear. Donald wore a beautiful cerise robe, but appeared falsely happy, frivolous; while Darlene seemed self-conscious and tense, and ran her arm through Donald's as they walked. Donald began strutting and laughed.

"Cut out the crap and get this show on the road!" Bea said. She quickly assembled them in the foyer and, out of the view of most people in the arena, lined them up in single file: Mavis first, then Donald, Cleo, Mack, and Darlene. Mistress of Ceremonies Bea would bring up the rear. She was sweating profusely—rivulets of perspiration ran down from underneath the red wig onto her face and made it glisten. She looked at Yeager once and his heart stopped, but although in the next moment she briefly stared at him, she seemed not really to see him, in her mind's involvement with more pressing matters.

Now she studied her line of performers, and, coming closer, in fierce whispers exhorted them—"Okay, let's be alive, now! Let's look *happy!*" She wiped perspiration from her eyes with a paper cocktail napkin—"You know how they are . . . they're always expectin' us to be happy," she said. "I never did understand why, but we're always supposed to be showin' our ivories. All right, then, let's show 'em!—skin 'em back *wide!*" She mopped her brow again—"God, another night like this an' I'm done for. . . . Lord, if that damn doctor that's always givin' me hell could see my blood pressure *now!*—I know it's outa sight. *Still* them honkies in that room there think we're so happy —yeah, always happy. They know *they* ain't, but think we are. Well, let's don't wise 'em up none! Let 'em think it—let 'em suffer! All right, then, let's look alive! Let's be *happy!* Okay, here we go!"

Mavis stepped off, and the others docilely followed. Yeager was weak from temporary relief. He stared at the expressions on their faces. Mavis was erect and proud— daredevilish. She walked with chin up and, swinging her arms slightly, retained her daring, cynical smile. At last his eyes went down the line to Darlene. She seemed stolid, indifferent to everything, and completely ignored him as she finally passed through the doors of the arena and was lost from view. Bea was the last to go in, and when she turned and closed the double doors, he soon heard the bolt in the lock slam into place.

"Let's git this stuff to the back," Bismarck was already saying—and picked up a bucket of melting ice cubes.

For a moment more Yeager could not move.

Chapter 7

THE next day was Saturday, and Yeager, after breakfast, waited impatiently in his room for any sounds indicating Darlene was up. But at 10:30 she still had not appeared. The morning was colder, though intermittently sunny, and the wobbly old radiator against the wall hissed and popped as it sent wet heat into his stuffy room. It was almost noon when he finally heard her out in the hall, and he opened his door at once. She was entering her room—and he was surprised to see her wearing her coat. Then he realized she was just coming home.

"Where . . . where have you been?" he said. "You've been out all night."

She glanced contemptuously at him and continued into her room—"So what?"

"I wanted to ask you something . . . before you go to bed."

"Go to bed—ha! I just got outa bed. Not here, though."

"Darlene! . . . But can I talk to you for a minute?" He followed her into her room. "Bismarck said you've got a Bible. Have you? Could I borrow it? . . ."

She turned around and stared at him. ". . . Bible! Yeah, I got a Bible. You need one, all right. You oughta been on some train by now, or a plane, gettin' as far away from this place as you could get. But no—you come askin' now for a Bible. Honest to God, I can't figure you out."

He looked away, and was soon whispering to himself again.

"If you was any kind of man," she said, "you'da been out of here five minutes after you found out what you'd got yourself into—'specially after I explained everything to you and warned you."

He had seemed in a daze but now aroused himself— "Shhhhh!" he said. "Someone will hear you."

"What difference does it make! Bea knows she's got you. She knows you're too damn scared to leave here. She even told that crowd last night that tomorrow night she was introducin' a new man—to take Chester's place. You're startin' tomorrow night. Did you know that?"

Desperate now, he quickly closed the door and confronted her. "Darlene! . . . let me have the Bible!"

She sighed and took off her coat. "You're so weak," she said. "It's kinda pitiful, really. I could slip you outa here later on—tonight—if you'd go. I told you that. But you ain't got the guts—you'd sooner stay around here and . . . and, yeah, join the show. Well, you ain't got long to make up your mind. Tomorrow night's the night. You shoulda heard them pecks clappin' and cheerin' at the news—they was crazy about Chester. Bea told 'em you was somethin' real special that she was bringin' all the way from St. Louis for 'em—that you'd performed for some awful big people there. They loved it. She ain't aimin' on disappointing 'em, either, I'll tell you that—*or* Kalandyk."

"I've stopped running," he said.

Her face crinkled from her vexation. "Willie, what kinda man *are* you!"

"Will you go to her, then, and tell her I can't do this? Plead with her?"

"Oh, no! Why, Christ, she'd wanta shoot me or somethin'. Or else she'd tell Kalandyk, which is worse. No, it wouldn't work. You got to lick this thing yourself. You got to get outa here—tonight! . . . I can slip you out."

He slowly shook his head. "Darlene, let me have the Bible."

"*Oh!*" she breathed angrily, and stepped to her night-table and took a small Bible out of the drawer. "This ain't going to help you," she said, still holding it.

He took it from her eagerly. "You don't know," he said, and sank at once into a chair. He opened the little Bible and began searching for a definite passage. "You don't understand," he murmured, almost to himself.

She was silent, awed, watching him. Yet she started once to speak, but at last did not.

He went on feverishly thumbing through the pages. "All night long," he said, "I thought and dreamt about my wife, Florrie. Mostly about her soul. I had awful dreams. I didn't give her a chance to pray, you know—there in the hotel—although she begged for it. She knew everything was over for her, all right, but I should have let her pray. Well . . ." His voice wavered, then failed as his lower lip quivered. But soon, blinking his eyes, he went on turning the pages.

"That was her name, was it?" Darlene, wide-eyed, stood over him. ". . . Flowery."

For a moment he rested the Bible on his kness and looked away. "Florrie," he whispered.

"You was crazy about her, all right—I can see that." The thought seemed to nettle her. But he was searching the pages now. She sighed again, sat down on the bed and, watching him, lit a cigarette.

". . . crazy? . . . crazy?" he soon murmured, his eyes still in the Bible. "Not the right word. But then maybe . . . maybe it is! Yes." He turned a few more pages. "I was crazy about Florrie, yes—if you mean demented . . . mad . . . unbalanced!"

"Oh, Willie, what're you sayin'! . . . what're you talkin' about!"

Head down in the book, he was oblivious. Suddenly he straightened up. "The passage . . . I have found it. Ah, here it is . . . Jesus and the whore." He read as if mesmerized.

Now she watched him with a trace of self-pride. "That's

a handy little Bible, all right, ain't it?" she said. He continued reading, but she went on—"A good-lookin' young
black minister gave it to me when I was in the hospital
... that was over a year ago. I still read it. I get good
thoughts out of it, too." She paused and drew on her
cigarette, waiting for him to listen. But completely ab-
sorbed in reading, he was still oblivious, his shoulders
rising and falling with his heavy breathing. "How ... how
did Florrie ever get mixed up with a damn peckerwood?"
she said. "Didn't she know white men are no good—
Jesus!"

His mouth opened as he finally looked at her, and for
the instant the reminder brought back all his searing rage
—before he sighed. But he did not answer her.

"I thought *I* was gonna die once," she said, in half
humorous soliloquy. For the moment the erratic sun was
flooding in at the two weather-grimed windows beyond
her bed, showing up the cluttered room in all its disarray
—a pair of her shoes lay carelessly on their sides before
the closet, and a little heap of cast-off lingerie rested on
the tufted stool in front of her dressing table mirror. But
the bed, unslept in, was still neatly made. "Dying ain't a
good feeling, I can tell you that," she said, smiling. "There
in the hospital my number was really up. I sure thought
so, anyhow." She mashed out her cigarette. "It's been
about a year and a half now—I hadn't come to this damn

house then yet—and I accidentally got pregnant. Like a
fool I tried to get rid of it myself . . ."

Yeager, who had resumed reading, looked up and
nodded gravely—"Yes, I know about it already."

". . . *Bea!*" Darlene's eyes blazed in anger. "That black
bitch Bea told you, didn't she!"

"Yes."

"That big bulldagger! I'll . . . I'll get even with her for
everything one of these days! What else did she say about
me?"

But he had begun reading again.

She watched him for a moment in a silent huff. "You
better read that Bible," she said. "You're sure gonna need
it."

He gazed up at her, his face full of emotion. "Go on,
tell me what happened, Darlene," he said very patiently.
"You can tell me."

"Oh, you ain't interested." She turned away.

"Yes, I am. I know what it is to have no one to talk
to. Go ahead—I'll listen." He placed the open Bible across
his knees again and waited.

She still pouted. But soon she lit another cigarette and
methodically blew out the match—reflecting, thinking.
"Well, in the first place," she said, "I didn't know tryin'
to give yourself an abortion could be so dangerous—a girl
I knew said she had—so I went on and done it. After the

third day, though, I had lost so much blood I was in shock, and dyin'—I didn't know it, but I was dyin'. When the people I was stayin' with found out what I'd done, they called a doctor right away. He didn't come, and after four hours they called two or three times more. Finally next morning around eight he showed up. When he found out what the situation was, he put me in the city hospital—fast. There three more doctors examined me and, quick, started givin' me blood transfusions—one quart right after another. But they thought it was too late—I was sinkin'. Then pretty soon this young black minister—he was real clean-cut lookin', like he'd just got outa school—came in the ward to see me, and set down in the chair by my bed and talked very quiet, very kind, to me. First he asked me if I was comfortable, if anything hurt me. I told him no I wasn't hurtin'. He asked me then if I had ever had 'a religious experience.' I didn't know what he was talkin' about—besides, I was so weak. He asked me another way —if I had ever been 'converted.' I said no. He said that was serious, because if the doctors were right I might be going into eternity soon. He said I oughta pray with him —pray not so much to live necessarily, but that my soul would be purged, would be clean."

Yeager watched her with an obsessive stare.

"But hell," she laughed, "I prayed to live! . . . I didn't wanta die. This nice educated young minister was prayin' for my soul, but I was prayin' for my body—to live! Sure, I was weak as a cat, but, oh, did I pray! And God heard me, too—he heard me and spared my life. Two weeks later, when I was leavin' the hospital, this young minister gave me that Bible you're holdin' and told me to always read it. I sure have, too. And I also been prayin' ever since —believe me." She grew wistful. ". . . indeed I have . . ."

Yeager stared down at the Bible. "I believed in prayer once," he said. "In fact, until very recently, I've even tried to pray since I've been in this house—although I knew it wouldn't do any good. But it always takes me back over the years . . . a long time, really—when I was in college for about three years. There I was taught some things I disregarded, or actually scoffed at, at the time—about religion. I was warned against it!" His eyes shone fanatically. "Yes, yes—I was! Yet most of my adult life, directly or indirectly, has been spent in religious work—I've written reams on religious subjects. But can it be now that I believe in none of it?—not even in prayer? . . ."

"What d'you want with a Bible, then?" Darlene said, displeased.

"Somehow I wanted to read again about Jesus and the harlot—here in the seventh chapter of St. Luke. How beautiful this passage . . . how moving. He forgave the woman and rebuked the Pharisee. I was hoping I could get some feeling of assurance from it—whatever little it may be—that Florrie, after all, was at least given the same remission as the woman in Luke; that I hadn't completely destroyed her chances of salvation . . . by not giving her any time there in the hotel to pray. But now I can only say that I don't know—for I myself have lost all faith. Maybe in the final seconds she was not disowned—that's my hope, anyway . . . for certainly I have been."

Darlene spoke with total conviction. "God don't disown *nobody*. Oh, He'd like for us to live a clean life, all right. But He knows—the world bein' like it is—that this ain't possible for everybody. If He was only interested in the so-called 'good' people, He wouldn't be half as great as He is—'cause the good people don't need much help. Besides, they're only good 'cause they're lucky and have had it better than most of us. But you take the people that's havin' it rough, the ones that's catchin' hell all the time, people that the world is down on—they're the ones that need Him. He won't turn His back on 'em either. He didn't disown me, did He? He sure didn't—He saved my life."

Yeager breathed deeply again, and gazed out the window. "Maybe . . . maybe He didn't disown her. . . ." he finally said.

Darlene almost stood up—"*Willie* . . . what happened? What made you do such an awful thing!"

A frigid calm seemed to come over him. He looked at

her pained, urgent, commiserating face. "I don't know what happened," he said. "I swear before God I don't. I only know what happened physically—but what caused it all is as mystifying to me as it would be to you if you knew all the facts. I was very good to her in some ways, but mentally cruel, maybe, in others—I realize it now. But we had just come here from New Waterford, and I was trying to get established—I was making progress, too. But there was always this feeling I had about her, that I'd had from the beginning, that she didn't really like me —much less love me—didn't even respect, or appreciate me. One night in bed she got angry at me and cried her eyes out—said I was an 'oddball.' It all worried me . . . tormented me . . . in everything I tried to do—until finally it got to be a mania. I'm sure I was impossible to live with sometimes—but not always, either. We had some good times together—she'd tell you that. She tried to help me, too—and went out and got a job as a cashier in one of the car-wash places this man, Rupert, owned . . . ah, that's how it got started."

"How what got started? . . ." Darlene, who had been staring at him, now twisted impatiently. "What happened! —Willie, why do you keep beatin' around the bush?"

He ignored her, and seemed merely to soliloquize, as if alone in the room. ". . . In the first place, she was too young for me." His voice was low, reflective. "I must admit in our case a difference of fourteen years was too great, but I didn't realize this originally—I was so completely out of my head about her. *She* did, though, I think —it took me a year and a half to talk her into marrying me. When you consider how poor her family was there in New Waterford, she shouldn't have been that hard to convince." He finally turned to Darlene, and his voice somehow came back to its normal level. "New Waterford was also my first wife's home town—she had died there two years before that. So I guess it was the old situation of a lonesome widower falling for a girl . . . but still I was only thirty-eight, and had a pretty good job on the staff of the black newspaper there—as church editor. On the other hand, she was an orphan, one of four, who lived with a penniless old aunt down not too far from the railroad tracks—actually almost next door to a fertilizer plant. So Florrie's life had been hard . . . hand-to-mouth, so to speak. Somehow she had gone to junior college, then gotten a job as a stenographer at this newspaper. That's of course how we met. I saw right off that, besides being in her own way good-looking, she had a lot of intelligence and determination. It was her looks, though, that the fellows around the office liked—especially her lovely legs. I of course was taken with her on all counts, and would get furious when these guys would kid me and call me 'Reverend'—because I was church editor—in her presence. Well anyway, after hounding her everyday on the sly, I finally got her to go out with me occasionally—to dinner, or a movie, or to some church affair on my beat. All this time, even though I tried not to, I was getting myself more and more involved, more worked up about her than ever. I was soon wild about her and wanted desperately to marry her. I finally told her this, so she wasn't in any doubt about my intentions."

Highly displeased, Darlene had by now almost turned her back on him. "You shoulda been in doubt about *hers,* though!" she said—scorn, jealousy, in her voice. "But don't that figure? . . . Oh, was you a square!"

"But she stalled me off," he said—he would not be distracted. "She put me off month after month. Sometimes she'd try to avoid the subject altogether—although maybe in a smiling or laughing way—but I could tell she was worried and upset, probably tormented by her own indecision . . . maybe by some terrible premonition of what would someday happen to her, I don't know. But I kept after her—I wouldn't give her any peace. Of course, I feel badly, guilty, about this now. Then one day I found out that the newspaper owner's son had taken her to a cocktail lounge. I hit the ceiling. I'm sure she preferred him a lot to me, but as it turned out he wasn't too interested in her. This, I'm certain, really disappointed her, for he was her one chance of escaping me. Then my berating her for going out with him coming on top of that was just too much for her—she was very despondent, and moped for two weeks. It took a lot of doing on my part to win her back—I almost lost her . . . and with no real rival at all. She was a strange, sensitive girl—impossible, really, to understand. Yet she was stubborn—she could be a real mule. I only knew, though, that I was in love with her and wanted to marry her. Nothing else mattered. It was acute. I was lovesick—but a quarrelsome fanatic too. Somehow I was burning up inside—consumed by some fire I could not put out or possibly cope with. It finally for awhile made me physically sick, then it . . ."

"All you're doin' now is reminiscin', Willie! You're livin' in the past—lettin' your mind go back to things that're dead and gone. I'm tired listenin' to it—all you wanta talk about is how much you was in love, and so forth . . . on, and on, and on. Yeah?—then how could you turn around and do that *awful* thing? You still won't face up to it! What I'm waitin' to hear is . . ." Her face showed her distress. "Oh, Lord!—I give up. . . ."

He said nothing.

"What happened, Willie?" She was quieter now, almost submissive.

His voice too was weak. ". . . she married me."

"What? . . ."

"She finally married me. And three months later I got

this new job here—with the Black Christian Publishing Company. I, of course, brought her with me. But getting settled in a new town can be expensive, and, although I certainly didn't ask her to, she went out, as I told you, and got this cashier's job at the car-wash place."

Darlene, still sitting on the bed, had kicked off her shoes. Now she brought her feet around up onto the bed and lay on her side, propped on her elbow, watching him.

He was sitting in the chair near her bed but would not look at her as he talked. "This white guy who owned the string of car-wash places—his name, as you know, was Noel Rupert—was quite a big shot around town, I later learned. He owned a lot of things—like the 'Spiders' pro basketball team, the Standard Ice Cream Company, and controlling interest in two or three other pretty good-sized businesses. I saw him one day when I went to pick up Florrie—he wasn't very tall, but was a flashy dresser, and drove big new cars all the time and threw a lot of money around. But he gave money to various charities too—some of them black. After Florrie had worked there for awhile, though—and this was before I'd ever seen him—I got a feeling, the strangest feeling, that she ought to quit the job and come home, or else maybe get a different job. I don't know why, but I felt it. I convinced myself at the time that it was because I wanted her to have children— but she wouldn't have had to stop work in order to get pregnant. Even she told me that. Yet whenever I'd suggest to her that she quit, she'd find excuses. She'd say she only wanted to work for another year—maybe not that long—and get a few new clothes. This went on for months. Finally one evening she did come home with a new coat— in a box so big she could hardly carry it. It was a beautiful, soft, cloth coat. She said she'd got it on sale at Ribner's for only $145.00. I expected her to be elated, as she was sometimes—almost like a child. But she wasn't at all this time. She seemed too offhand about it—and a little tense, I thought. Then a couple of days later on the back stoop I accidentally saw the Ribner's sales slip—wet and sticking to the inside of the garbage can. Sales tax included, the coat had cost $367.50."

". . . Good Lord!" Darlene said.

Yeager frowned, in a perverse, perplexed, way—"It started me to worrying, really worrying. But I was afraid to say anything to her about it—for I knew she'd be good and mad. Then, too, I thought I could be wrong about how she got that kind of money. So I tried to forget it. But I couldn't, and then I—"

There were two hard raps on the door. And Bea opened the door and walked in.

Darlene spun around and sat up on the bed, then pushed her feet into her shoes. But Yeager, dour, taciturn, kept his seat, the Bible still in his hands.

"Say! . . . whut the hell's goin' on in here!" Bea laughed —there was the heavy smell of whiskey on her breath. "You-all must be rehearsin' for tomorrow night! Where's Donald, then?—Haw! You better go git *him!"* She was unsteady on her feet.

Suddenly Darlene jumped up and stood before her— "Bea, Willie can't do it! He can't go through with it. Give him a break—you'll find somebody else in a week or two, somebody that'll be okay. But not him—God, not him!"

Bea, in her housecoat and flowing red wig, seemed for a moment not to comprehend; she was unable to move; her eyes stared in incredulity. "Darlene, you're drunk agin," she finally breathed. "God-damn it to hell, you're . . ."

"No, I ain't, either! I'm tryin' to talk some sense in your head! I gotta funny feelin' we're all skatin' on thin ice. Don't make this man do this! He's so scared now he's half crazy. You can't tell what he'd do up there tomorrow night —with that room jammed full of people and all the excitement goin' on. It could be curtains for everybody! Don't make him do it, Bea!—Don't!"

Bea's mouth was hanging open, yet she seemed unable to speak. Then a guttural yell came up out of her—*"Why, you little bitch, you!* . . . I'll whip your ass agin!" She lunged forward and her huge fist went back to swing.

In the instant Yeager was on his feet and jumped between them. He pushed Darlene aside. At last he faced

Bea, the Bible in his hand. "She was only trying to help me," he said. "I know it's no use. But don't you have any pity at all in your heart? I'm caught—you can see I'm caught. Don't you have any *pity?*"

Bea, gaping in dumb unbelieving outrage, reeled back against the door. Finally, she placed both hands across her breast, as if in supplication, and twice tried to speak, but maudlin rage choked her words. At last she said, weakly, ". . . pity." For a moment she could say no more. Then again—"Pity. . . . Whut in God Almighty's name are you talkin' about?" Finally she yelled it at the top of her lungs —"*Who ever had any pity on me!*" She began beating her breast with both fists—"*Me! Me! Me! Me! Who?*" Suddenly she rushed at him and jutted her massive face into his—"*Look!*" she screamed. "Looka here!" She jabbed her forefinger at her face—"The kids in school called me '*Ape'!*" Then with a savage swipe she tore off her wig— "Looka there! Lookit me! . . . Men have always run from me like I had the syph! Iris's daddy worked on a garbage truck, but when he got me bigged, even *he* wouldn't marry me! . . . and you come talkin' to me about *pity!*" She stopped for a moment, mouth open, gasping, panting— "Pity! . . . My ticker's so God-damn bad, and my blood pressure's so outa sight, I can keel over any minute! . . . and be dead the next—*dead!* And you come talkin' to me about pity! . . . *Well, no motherfucker ever had any pity on me!*

Right now couldn't I have Mack Thomas throw your ass out in the street while I'm phonin' the police?—huh? Couldn't I? Why, they'd pick you up 'fore you got two blocks. And you come askin' me ain't I got any pity!" She swung around to Darlene and shouted—"You git up there to my room! . . . I ain't done with you yet, you connivin' little whore, you! You been out all night with your legs hoisted up in the air and then come in here tryin' to break up my business!—the business that keeps you eatin'! Git outa here and up to my room before I put my fist in your eye!" She lunged again at Darlene, who quickly side-stepped her and retreated to the door.

"Go, Darlene," Yeager said—"Go on."

Darlene went out.

He and Bea once more confronted each other. Her eyes were wild and her breathing labored as she still clutched the wig in her hand. Finally he said to her—"I have no quarrel with you now. I have no quarrel with anybody. I'll do whatever you say."

"You make me sick—always soundin' like a God-damn preacher. Put that Bible down! You damn right you'll do what I say—*tomorrow night!* Git in your own room!"

He placed the Bible on the nighttable and went out ahead of her. She went up the hall toward her room and Darlene.

As he entered his room he seemed somehow weightless

again, and approached his window as if it were an open door—to step out of, or soar through. And when he had to stop, with the toes of both shoes against the wall beneath the window, he still made a feeble, quailing effort to peer far down from the third-floor height of his position to examine the backyard below. But he saw that it was not frozen—only cold mud—and he felt resentful. There was the shadowed impression of the mud as undignified, defiling to his pitifully smashed body, and he turned away in horror—again to take refuge in recent, more habitual thinking.

He went then to the bed, reached under the pillow, and took out a gleaming daggerlike knife he had filched from the kitchen that morning. Its touch was cool and soothing to him, and his weightlessness disappeared into an aura of overcoming all. He quickly hid the knife in the middle dresser drawer under the newspaper liner and at last lay down on his back across the bed and vaguely stared at the ceiling—how indistinct his feelings now, yet how ever-hovering his resolve; how quiet, solemn, the fateful afternoon. Soon he slept.

Chapter 8

THAT evening, rather than repeat the ordeal of eating in the dining room with all the others, Yeager went to the kitchen beforehand, got a sandwich from old Jessie, and brought it back to his room. His mind had cleared now, his purpose become firm resolve. Yet his hand shook as he ate. Later, shortly before nine o'clock, Darlene came to his room. She was spiritless, subdued, as she sat down on his bed with a sigh.

"You went off and left the Bible in my room," she said.

"I don't need it any more." His voice was edgy—"Did Bea try any rough stuff?"

"No, just kept ravin' and carryin' on like a maniac. She's good and drunk now—sleepin'. Yes, you do need that Bible —you need it now more'n ever."

He only sat squinting up at his glaring light overhead.

"*Willie,* what're you gonna do?"

He seemed surprised—"What am I going to do? That's all settled, you know that."

"What's all settled?—I don't know nothing. Are you gonna get outa here tonight?"

He studied her face. "No, I've told you I've stopped running."

"Oh, God!" she said bitterly. "Well, you may change your tune after that skull session in Bea's room tomorrow. You'll get an eyeful and an earful then, chapter and verse. They're gonna rehearse with you, take you through the whole routine, for tomorrow night. You may have a different notion then!"

"What are you trying to do, make it harder for me?"

"I'm tryin' to make it better for you! Tonight—*now*—is your last chance."

"My last chance is gone, Darlene. I feel it—I know it."

"It don't have to be! Bea's in bed, drunk." Darlene stood up. "Get your hat and coat—I'll let you out the back door, right now!"

Yeager only shook his head.

"Oh, Willie, why have you give up so?"

"The odds are too great—I'm talking about the odds of life. Actually, they've always been too great, only I didn't realize it before. But few people do, and even die not realizing it. Being the kind of man I am, though, has made the odds against me even greater, prohibitive—really a sure thing."

Distressed and exasperated, she sank down on the bed again. "Willie, I've asked you before, what kinda man *are* you? Did you ever ask yourself that?"

"Many times. More than ever in the awful hours I've spent in this room. I still don't know. That's part of the whole riddle too."

"You was in church work, and you seem like a nice man, all right—'till I think of . . . 'till I remember . . . oh, that awful thing you—" Darlene stopped, fear in her face. "Only a monster-man coulda done that, Willie . . . ain't that right?"

He spoke thoughtfully. "Yes, for I knew everything I was doing. And I wanted to do it."

Her hand went to her mouth—"Oh!"

"It was a new feeling," he said. "Yet that night I considered it a natural condition of life. It was easy. It's what happens when you finally wake up to what life's done to you, and really understand that, all along, the odds against you were absurd. Sure, I was a monster, because I'd gotten wise."

Darlene gasped—"Wise!"

"Yes. I'd gotten wise like Noel Rupert. I'd become a predator."

". . . .What!"

"An animal that lives by destroying others. Rupert was the prototype."

"Oh, Willie, what're . . ."

Suddenly Yeager stood up, trembling. Yet his face was cold, cruel. "He was, that is, until I stepped out of that hotel room closet with a hunting knife." He spoke now with nervous, jerky little gestures, though not raising his voice. "All along, the odds had been against Rupert too, but he didn't know it, either. Something tricked him! Call it fate or any other name you want. Whatever it was had him fire one of his car washers for being drunk on the job too much. That was *it!* That was all it took—just a little thing like that. One day soon afterwards, I ran into this silly joker, the car washer, in a dry cleaning place where I'd taken a couple of suits—he was drunk even then— and, knowing who I was, he started making wisecracks. He laughed and said I'd better start watching the 'big boss,' the 'great white father,' or throw some nails under his tires, or something, to slow him down, before somebody got hurt. 'Watch him, man,' he said, and gave his crazy, drunken laugh again—'He don't let no grass grow under his feet. He might not like *us* so much but he sure likes our women. Keep an eye on him, man.' Then he came up close, grinning in my face with his foul breath, and whispered, 'He keeps a room in the old Webster Hotel, down on Ignatius Boulevard, and it ain't for sleepin', either—he's got a home, and a wife and kids, where he sleeps. I tell you, man, *watch* that honky!' He laughed and soon staggered out. I should have jumped up and fought him, but I was so stunned I just sat there—it seemed I'd lost all feeling in my body. So you see, my luck, just like Rupert's, had finally run out . . . ah, and Florrie's too. . . ." At last Yeager's voice trailed off and his arms fell helplessly to his sides as he sat down in the chair again.

Darlene, in her rapt involvement, could only stare.

The pained grimace came on his face now as he fidgeted in the chair. "From then on it was terrible . . . terrible!— it can't really be described. I couldn't sleep, or eat, or work . . . or even think. I was petrified—no matter where I was, I just stood or sat and looked in space. I rolled and tossed so, night after night, that Florrie began then to get uneasy—at breakfast I'd catch her watching me. This went on for at least ten days. I was out of my mind. Finally, I decided on trying to shadow her. It didn't work, of course —it was really silly, ridiculous, of me. Then I thought up the idea of watching that hotel, the Webster Hotel, that this guy had told me about. I soon found out with no trouble that Rupert kept a room there, all right. Then one afternoon when, for the nth time, it seemed, I was sitting in my car watching the place, I saw him go in. Yes, yes, I saw him! . . . What luck! What a thrill . . . what a joy it was! I started watching the place in earnest then . . . until my job began to suffer—already the publisher had warned me twice. But I was desperate, obsessed, and kept up this watch whenever I possibly could for three weeks. Darlene, I beg you to believe me—you must believe me! —when I tell you that no human being ever suffered more than I did in those three weeks. Hell itself can hold no terrors for me now." Excited, his eyes glowing, he

jumped up and stood before Darlene seated on the bed.
"Finally . . . then finally—oh, at last, at long last!—one
rainy Tuesday afternoon I saw Florrie get off a bus and go in
that hotel." He turned his back on her now and brought up
both hands as a mask to his face, to his eyes, yet could not cry,
although his whole body shook. *"And that was it!"* he
blurted at last, his dry eyes now popping at her. "Right
away I started the car and drove off."

"Drove off!"

"Yes! There was nothing I could do—or wanted to
do—right then. I wanted to plot, to plan, to perfect,
everything. I wanted to toy with them. I had this com-
pulsion, this necessity, to make it something special—a
great event. I was cold and murderous by then—cunning,
calculating." Standing over Darlene, his eyes afire, he
struck his breast with his fist—"I had gotten wise! Now *I*
was the predator!"

"Willie, you're some other man," Darlene said in
wonder, though sadly. "Seems like I don't know you—I
don't know you at all. There must be *two* of you—honest
to God. When Bea and I brought you here that mornin',
you was shakin' like a leaf, and whinin' like a baby. You
was scared to death. *Now* look at you. Why, sure—you're
a monster-man."

In his excitement he seemed not to hear her. "But then
I couldn't think of any plan!" he said, wrenching his body

around and staring madly behind him. *"That* was my problem now! I couldn't think, period. And, as I mentioned, I think Florrie already sensed something. So I tried to be as casual and natural as I could at home. Yet it made my flesh crawl to have her even touch me. In bed one night, though, she faked a try at getting me to have sex with her—I think maybe to test me, or to reassure herself that things were really still okay with us. I couldn't afford not to go along—I certainly didn't want to give her any reason to get more suspicious. So I finally managed to go through with it, but it was dreadful, horrible—the way I felt . . . thinking of her and Rupert in bed, naked, in that hotel room and all the things they did to each other. I kept wanting to kill her right then . . . strangle her with my bare hands, or do anything—I just didn't want her to live. She was never to know how close to death she came that night, of course, although I'm sure she sensed something was very wrong, but couldn't pinpoint it. I knew then I had to do something fast—that I couldn't go on like this. Still again, for a couple of more nights—although we never had sex any more—I found myself thinking of killing her, in some way, right there in the house. But I soon saw this didn't make any sense when I thought of Rupert . . . I knew now I wanted to catch them both together . . . preferably in the hotel room, if I could. I was beside myself, on a brand new plane of

experience, almost slavering like a dog with rabies. I was
bold too, and next day went to the hotel, took a bellhop
off to the side, and finally got him to take twenty dollars
to smuggle a key to Rupert's room out for an hour—the
time it would take me to go get it duplicated. This was
the way I got a key of my own, and I carried it around
in my pocket while I shadowed the hotel off and on for
still another two weeks, but to no avail; there was nothing
doing, at least at the times of the day I could get away
from the office long enough to go sit out in my car and
watch the hotel. Meantime, day in, day out, I was going
through the tortures of hell itself—I could hardly eat
anything at all, and it began to show up in what you see
now, a bad loss of weight. During this time I remember
I was trying to write an inspirational piece for our publication on the occasion, told in the New Testament, when
Jesus fed the multitude with the five loaves and two fishes
—do you remember that? The others at the office kidded
me and said I should have been there to get some of that
free food myself. For I'd already gotten skinny as a rail.
On top of that, I started feeling sorry for myself, and at
the office would lock myself in one of the toilet stalls in
the men's washroom and try to cry. I wanted, I needed,
to cry my eyes out. I had to have relief someway. But I
could not cry a single tear. I was on the verge of panic
now, of insanity—I felt I would suddenly explode like a

bomb. Yet, so far as I'd been able to determine, Florrie had stopped going to the hotel altogether—I even went back to this bellhop, my third call, to find out if Rupert still had his room there. He checked, and said he did. I didn't know what to do then. I was stopped—cold."

Darlene bristled. "She smelled a mouse, that's what!"

He gave her a fevered, absent look. "It was then I began to concoct one of the wildest, most harebrained schemes any lunatic ever thought up! . . . I'd make it possible for her to get out *at night!* Yes—at night! I would tell her I had to go to Cleveland or some place for a couple of days—to cover a meeting, say, of religious leaders for the publication. Then when I began thinking about it, and really making plans, I realized how crazy, how impossible, it was. There were so many 'ifs' in it—what, for instance, if Rupert was getting bored, or couldn't get away at night? . . . or Florrie got suspicious and checked with my office? . . . or was scared to leave the house at night for fear I might phone from Cleveland? There were numberless chances for things to go wrong, and I soon realized what a farce it all was. But then I began to ask myself what alternatives I had. I had none, of course. And all the time fate was pushing me. It had emboldened me. Yes, yes—it was fate! Some people would laugh, but now, as I said before, I believe in fate. I acknowledge it! . . . bow to it. Hasn't it ruled my whole life, my nauseating life? . . . my nightmare! Why shouldn't I salute it! So in spite of everything, of any and all chancy possibilities, that Sunday night I packed my bag and told Florrie it was sudden, but that I had to go to Cleveland next morning to cover this two-day meeting—that I had a 10:00 AM flight and would be back on Wednesday. I watched her reaction. Again, I thought, she took it too casually. But soon she smiled and said she'd miss me. It made my heart turn over. Then for some reason she wouldn't look at me again—she seemed cold, fearful, tense. Was it a sense of foreboding? I'll never know, of course. Next morning I left the house, drove to the railroad station instead of the airport, and deposited my bag in a coin locker. Then I tried to read magazines, had lunch, and later went to two movies, hoping the day would not drag; yet it seemed interminable, for I was suffering so. But as soon as it got dark I took up my painful watch again outside the hotel. Sitting there in the car in the dark, I was suddenly jarred by the thought that they could have come there during the day and already be gone—while I stupidly sat watching a movie. Yet I had no choice but go through with what I felt so hopeless about now. And I did.

"At nine o'clock—in the dark it was snowing lightly—I left the car, crossed the street, and slipped in a side door of the hotel lobby. Things were pretty quiet except that three men were just checking in, so I went straight to the automatic elevator and went up to the fourth floor. Rupert's room was No. 416, near the end of the hall; when I reached it I took out my key and entered with no trouble at all. I would have been surprised at my own boldness if I hadn't been too numb to think, yet I was really scared to death. The hotel itself is not the best, but when I put on the light I saw that this room was a pretty snug affair—with a color television set, a bearskin rug in front of a false fireplace, a shelf of paperback books, and a bar. But the real shock came when I looked in the clothes closet. The first thing I saw was Florrie's little turquoise sweater—I knew it so well because it had little sequins across the front. I was sick—sick with rage. I turned out the light right away and, gripping the knife— oh yes, I had brought one—sat down on the floor of the closet, with the closet door slightly ajar, and waited. I knew I had to be ready to act quickly if they came, for the closet would be the first place they'd come to—to hang up their coats. So I was ready. But it was torture—the waiting, and waiting, and waiting. Yet by midnight no one had come. Nor by one o'clock. Then it must have been around two that, from sheer exhaustion, I dozed off to sleep—and woke up only when dawn showed through the windows. I jumped up and sneaked out right away. It had all been a silly, miserable mistake. A failure." Yeager, as if still exhausted, now went over and sank into the chair.

Darlene was staring with burning eyes. "Willie, I've heard enough. I don't wanta hear any more. Keep the rest to yourself, 'cause I can see you *like* to tell it! You do! ... it takes you back to what you done. Ain't that right? I know you ain't exactly braggin' about it, but ... but twice already you have mentioned the knife—the knife you had in the closet."

"Yes, but after they didn't show up that night, I went next day and got another knife—a different knife."

"Another ... ?"

"I had brooded so ... yes, yes ... another—a *bigger* knife. I had brooded so over her betrayal that I decided that if I did catch her, I would take harsh, extreme measures. It would be a ritual, something definite and impressive; she would be sacrificed to me and the way she had made me suffer in a kind of penance offertory, a *coup de grace*. So I went and bought the hunting knife."

"Oh, Willie ... what? It ain't easy to believe you're that kinda person! But you are! Willie, now I see you as you are!—you're a *devil!*"

He was indifferent. "Who knows what I am? I'm a product, like everybody, of what's behind me—my past— and fate. Yes, fate had decreed that the drama be played out to its end; so I never lacked determination. The proof is that while everything had been a flop that first night, the following night went perfectly—just perfectly. But my nerves were completely wrecked by now; I had carelessly, thoughtlessly, left my car lights on—of all times!—when I went in the hotel the first night. Of course, when I came out next morning the battery was dead and I had to leave the car where it was. I didn't care; my mind was not on cars; I walked the streets that second day like a mad man, waiting, hungering, thirsting, once more for night to come. Strangely, I somehow felt that when it did I would not be disappointed, but the feeling was temporary, a hallucination, for I was yet to have to sweat before I experienced that perfect night—the most perfect night of my life! But my nerves worried me; they were completely gone, shattered; I feared now I might weaken in my purpose. Of all the times in my life, I needed strength tonight. So, although I almost never drank, I bought a half-pint of bourbon whiskey and took it with me to sip on while I waited out my ordeal in the closet in Rupert's dark room. This second night I was in the room by eight o'clock. It was the same old vigil—the awful, the terrible waiting. Again I suffered the tortures of hell, I tell you!—physical as well as mental. My legs in the cramped closet began to ache and the air got so close and stuffy I thought I would suffocate. I sipped the whiskey but as time dragged on, and on, and on, I lost all hope and began to despair— it was the second and *last* night, you know . . . there would be no third. So by midnight I was trying to cry again—but

of course could not. Then I prayed . . . do you hear me?—
although I no longer believed in prayer, I prayed. Afterwards I sipped more whiskey, but the minutes dragged
into hours, the hours into what seemed a lifetime; passing
units of time, whatever, seemed endless, eternal. I was
finally overcome by this feeling of hopelessness and let-
down . . . and soon I began to get sluggish, apathetic. Now,
remembering the night before, I feared sleep. Then I
realized I was already fighting sleep. One o'clock came,
though, and something happened to me. I can't very well
describe it. All my drowsiness disappeared, almost at once.
An alertness came over me I had never experienced before.
It seemed too as if my blood were suddenly coagulating,
preparing the body for some crucial, dangerous, mortal
event; and I also noticed I was breathing faster. Ah . . . it
was then . . . it was *then*—that very moment!—that I
heard talking out in the hall. My heart stopped. The two
approaching voices, a man's and a woman's, could still
have been those of total strangers to me, yet I somehow
knew—I *knew*—they were not! I now made a mighty
effort to stand up in the dark closet, but failed on my first
attempt. I succeeded next time—the very moment I heard
the key in the door. *They had come!"* Yeager began a
violent quivering and shaking, and spittle formed on his
lips again. Leering madly, he gave a violent twist around
in the chair as if still trying to see behind him. ". . . They

had come," he repeated hoarsely.

Darlene jumped up off the bed, renewed fear in her face under the glaring ceiling light—"I don't wanta hear any more, I tell you! Willie!—I don't!"

He struggled to his feet and gently pushed her back down, as she gave him a frightened, uncomprehending look. "I had been in that dark, narrow closet for five hours."—he eased down in the chair again. "My legs were past hurting; they were numb—dead. I began to wonder now if I could walk—if I could function! I was appalled, frantic . . . once more I prayed! . . . that I could function! Then the thought hit me that it might be Rupert—but with some *other* woman! In the instant that doubt was settled—the door had barely been opened when I heard Florrie's quiet laugh. My heart sickened at the sound. They came in and Rupert put on the light, then locked the door. He was a little drunk, it seemed, and very playful—Florrie was laughing a lot, too. Of course, I expected them to bring their coats to the closet, and I tried to be ready. But instead they went past me to the other side of the room, and I could see them better now. He was breathing hot in her face, and then they grappled and kissed moaningly in front of the mirror. Soon he tore off her coat and undressed her, and then himself. But *still* I waited . . . Oh, God! . . . *Oh, God!*" He dove his face in his hands. The room was quiet now, as Darlene, near tears, turned away. But

soon he raised his head again. His eyes were red but still
dry. He could barely speak—"Then, both of them naked,
again panting, moaning, in their embraces, they fell on the
bed together, and that was all the time I could bear to give
them. I couldn't have stayed in that closet another second
and heard her whining and puling under his stiff, white
prick. The time had come! . . . the end for them! And for
me too—*our* end! Rupert seemed only incidental, minor,
to me now. I killed her first. She begged for time to pray,
but I told her to pray in hell where I'd see her soon. I've
thought since that I should have saved her till the last, but
I didn't. So instead I killed him last—yet somehow without really hating him, although he died pleading for his
life, and for mercy on his wife and two little girls. But
Florrie was already dead then, so nothing mattered after
I saw that she was finally dead. She had died hard, and he
panicked at the sight of all the blood, knowing the same
was coming to him."

Darlene covered her face with her hands. ". . . *Oh!*"
she said, and would not look at him. "The devil had come
up to earth, Willie! . . . *you* was him!"

"A curious—an ironical—thing happened," Yeager
said, more calmly now. "When the struggle was over,
when he finally went down, was dead, he fell across her
on the bed and lay in almost the exact position he'd
eventually have been in if I hadn't interrupted them. This

upset me, and I threw him off of her and onto the floor. There was blood everywhere—even high up on the walls. But now the moment had come. With the big hunting knife still in my hand, I went to Florrie. I soon found out I had been wise in buying a much heavier knife, for I couldn't possibly have done now without it. As it was, it took me almost five minutes. Afterwards I got Rupert off the floor and threw him back on top of her; that is, on top of what was left. His eyes were still wide open. I wrapped what *I* had then in a piece of thick brown paper I found on the closet shelf. The piece of paper had contained a bundle of laundry and the printing on it said: 'Sidney Winter Laundry, Inc.—Your Things Will Come Back Whiter Than Snow'." Then Yeager sighed, lay back wearily in the chair, and was very quiet. At last he said emptily, "I'm tired of running now. As Bea said down in front of this building the morning you two brought me here: 'This is the end of the line'."

Darlene seemed in shock—unable to speak. She could only get up and stand directly in front of him. "You gotta pay up," she finally said. "You might as well get ready for it . . . you gotta pay for these sins. It won't be long comin', either. But you sure can't mean *this*—this house—is the end of the line." She gave an awkward little shudder. "What a hell of a place to end up at, then. Do you know what you're sayin', Willie? *Do* you? If you're so finished, if this is the end of the line, then why don't you walk outa here and take your medicine like a man?—and not go on hangin' around here sinkin' even lower, and lower, and lower. If you don't get outa this house tonight, you're gonna end up in the show. But you know this already—that's what makes it so hard for me to understand you. You know damn well what's goin' to happen to you here—and you'll get still more pa'ticulars on it tomorrow at the skull session up in Bea's room." But now she eyed him carefully—"Y'know what, though? . . . sometimes I think you *wanta* be in the show. Willie, did you ever think of that?—huh? Without realizin' it, you may be taken with the idea. . . . you might not know yourself as well as you think you do. Turn it over in your mind—you have already said here tonight you didn't know, yourself, what kind man you was. . . . didn't you say it?—indeed you did. Then how can you be sure?—*if* you're sure. Yeah, you just might be taken—secretly *burnin'*—with the idea. You never thought of that, did you? You're a strange bird, Willie. You're weird. You're weirder right now than anybody we got in that show—you don't know it but it's the truth. And foxy old Bea's probably seen it all along—from the beginnin' . . . I'll bet she has, queer as she is herself. I didn't see it, though—you had me fooled . . . ha, you and your religious work. Maybe I'm wrong but I think I got your number now. Still, I *hope* I'm wrong. That's why

I'm beggin' you for your own good to leave this house—tonight!"

Yeager seemed impervious, his mind elsewhere. "You're talking nonsense," he finally said. "Fantasy. You'll understand everything in due time. I'm not leaving this house—and of course I'm not going in the show." A desolate, agonized expression went over his face.

Darlene stood staring in bewilderment, then, finally near tears, she sank down on the bed again. ". . . You could go," she said, ". . . and . . . and maybe take me with you." She bit her quivering lip.

He leaned forward in the chair and stared at her—astonished. "Darlene . . . Darlene!" For a moment he could say no more. "Do you know what you're saying? My God! I'm a murderer! . . . do you realize that? I'm wanted for two horrible murders. If I go out there, I'll be taken. And if you're with me, you will too—for trying to help me escape. Can't you see that?"

She looked at the floor for a moment. ". . . I wouldn't care," she said.

"Oh, that's crazy!"

"It ain't crazy."

"What would you stand to gain?—nothing."

"I'd be gettin' outa here, wouldn't I?—outa this house. That's somethin', ain't it?"

Remembering, he curled his lip in scorn. "I thought

you *loved* the life you live here. That's what you told me the other night in your room."

"And you didn't believe it, neither—any more'n I did." Now her words came with more difficulty—"I *have* thought more about leavin', though . . . since you've been here . . . in talkin' with you. You made me see it more'n I had before . . . and feel it too." She looked away before she murmured—"I . . . I never had a man to talk to me before like you have. Every man I ever knowed only wanted to climb in the bed with me."

"Maybe I've wanted to do that too, Darlene. I'm no different from the others."

She thought for a moment. "You seem like you are, though. I thought maybe you liked *me* a little, not just my body. I guess I was wrong—I know what an awful life I have lived, and that no good man will ever want me. I know that." She would not look at him. For a moment both were silent.

"Darlene, when you say 'good man,' you are not referring to me, are you?"

She still would not look at him. ". . . Yes," she finally said.

He took a deep breath, but his eyes would not leave her face.

Suddenly she aroused herself. "Willie, we could leave here right now! . . . in ten minutes. We could be clear outa town by the time anybody found out! . . ."

He sadly shook his head. "What would we use for money?—I've only got about ninety dollars with me, and no way now to get any more. And how much have you got?"

". . . about two hundred," she said, dejection in her voice.

"Don't you see?—and when our little money ran out, what would we do then?"

"I can *always* make a livin'." She spoke with conviction.

"Yes, I know—and I'd be your pimp, eh? That would be helping you, wouldn't it?—don't be silly."

She absently pulled a raveled thread from the sleeve of her dress, then for a moment stared up directly into the blinding-bright light. At last she closed her eyes as she said, "I wouldn't care . . . I wouldn't care as long as you liked me. I never had anybody to like me. If you told me everyday you liked me, it would be all right."

"Oh, Darlene!" He was grimacing and wringing his hands again. "The answer is still, No! I've put all choices behind me now—I'm staying . . . I'm staying . . . for a little while . . ." The desolate, far-off expression came on his face once more.

She was cold and forbidding as she stood up—"Then, you're lower'n I am. . . . You're lower'n I've *ever* been!"

"Darlene, it won't be long . . . you'll understand."

But she had opened the door and was already stalking

out.

He kept his seat—for he had already begun to think of tomorrow.

Chapter 9

Y EAGER awoke the next morning to the far-off pealing of church bells—and realized it was Sunday. He got up and, gathering his paraphernalia, went in the bathroom and took a slow, hot bath; then shaved. It had rained during the night, and when he returned to his room the sky was still black and angry, and soon it began to pour rain again. When he went to his window, the water was coming down in driving sheets and the alley below was a sea of mud and rubbish. He saw a mongrel dog, filthy and wet, foraging for food in the backyard next door. And an all-night drunk was stumbling home down the alley, oblivious of his soaked, flapping clothing. Strangely the noise of the thunder and downpour seemed somehow to bring the church bells nearer.

Then shortly after ten o'clock he suddenly heard much movement and talking up the hall. Cracking his door slightly to hear better, he recognized the voices of Bea and Mavis—Bea was nervously guffawing, Mavis giggling. There was also a third voice—a man's. It was unfamiliar to him, but a white man's speech, he could tell that. "No, I'm not kidding," the man, apparently in good humor, was saying—"I want some breakfast . . . some bacon and eggs."

Both women laughed again, Bea nervously. ". . . Okay Bertie," she said, "but you *coulda* give us a little notice, looks like. We ain't always prepared for big-shot company, y'know—and on Sunday mornin'. Haw! Haw! Haw! Suppose I ain't got any food in the house?—Mavis, go back there and tell Jessie, ha, we got rich company for breakfast. But like I always say: 'What Bertie wants, Bertie gits.' Haw! Haw! Haw! Go on, Mavis."

In a moment Yeager heard Mavis hurry past his door on her way back to the kitchen, and very soon there was general commotion and activity throughout the house— as if some important dignitary had suddenly arrived. Also Iris began running up and down the hall, yelling, laughing, showing-off, until Mack Thomas ordered her to stop it. Soon, across the hall, Yeager heard someone knock on Darlene's door, and then Donald called softly to her: "Darlene!—get up! D'you hear? . . . Bertie's up front. D'you hear me?—Kalandyk's here!"

Yeager already had guessed as much, but still he froze hearing that surname. Then in a few minutes Bea came barging in his room—wearing her housecoat and flowing red wig. Again, she seemed suffused with anger the instant she saw him, and spoke warningly: "Now, listen—Kalandyk's here. He just come in unexpectedly, and is goin' to eat breakfast with us. I want you there—no stayin' in your room this mornin'. I told him on the phone yesterday

I had a new man, and I think he wants to see you. He's the boss, y'know. So get ready for breakfast. He's gonna size you up, of course—that's probably the reason he come. Or else he's been out all night, I don't know which. But watch your step, 'cause he's gonna be lookin' you over, but good. He ain't easy to fool, either—he's plenty sharp, I'll tell you, and has been around. I told him I got you from St. Louis. You ever been to St. Louis?"

Yeager was bitter, malicious. "Once," he said, "and for one whole day."

Bea seemed on the point of exploding again, but contained herself. "Well, you'll have to fake it, then—or else keep him away from the subject."

He made no reply.

"This ain't no plaything!" she said angrily—"for you *or* for me. Remember that. It's serious—this man don't play. So be ready in about a half-hour—and, for once in your life, do some talkin'! Kalandyk is smart, cagey. He'll be thinkin' about only one thing—how you're gonna fit into his business. But he'll be thinkin' plenty about that. Lord God, if he only knowed who you *really* was!—I git the shakes and my pressure goes higher'n ever every time I think about it." She left—as he cursed her under his breath.

Impulsively now, he crossed the hall and knocked on Darlene's door—"It's me . . . Willie," he said. "Breakfast will soon be ready—are you coming?"

"Sure, I'm comin'!" she snapped.

". . . Knock, then, will you?—we'll go together."

"No, we won't, either! And get away from that door."

"Darlene! . . ."

There was no further answer, and he finally returned to his room.

By 10:45 everyone was standing around in the dining room, waiting—except Bea and Kalandyk, who were still conferring up in Bea's room. There was orange juice at each place, and Bismarck was scurrying around the table distributing silverware, followed by Iris with the paper napkins. Hungry Mack Thomas stood off by himself looking forlorn and impatient, and kept his eyes on the kitchen door. Cleo was talking to glum Darlene, as Yeager stood apart absently watching the goldfish in the little aquarium over against the far wall. The fish, almost as large as perch, had great distended bellies and swam about sluggishly among the pebbles and slimy foliage in the tank. Soon Donald, who had been watching him, stepped up beside him, and, sticking up his nose as he too viewed the fish, whispered, "Don't they look nasty? I don't like fish at all —I won't eat 'em!" He gave his high, fluttering, tense laugh. Yeager nodded quickly, furtively, and left; then went over and stood beside Darlene, who ignored him.

At last Bea came in with the guest. Kalandyk resembled

a slightly plump, but not paunchy, oldish Rudolph Valentino—with even the long, sharp-pointed sideburns. His feet were small and very neat, and his complexion dark, ruddy, as if from much red wine. His hands were delicate, well-formed, and nervous. Entering, he smiled thinly, showing perfect white teeth, as he spoke to them all.

"Set here, Bertie." Bea placed her hand on the back of her own chair at the head of the table.

"No, Bea—that's your place," he said.

"Only when *you* ain't here, Bertie, baby," she laughed. "Set down now." Then she sat down at his right and looked around sternly at the others—"Okay, kids, set down." At that moment she saw Yeager—and swallowed. "Oh, Bertie! . . . yeah—that's Willie, there. Come up here, Willie."

Yeager stiffened, then stood coolly looking at her. She glared primeval violence at him. At last, but taking his time, he went up to the head of the table where Kalandyk sat.

Kalandyk looked up at him carefully, curiously, as they shook hands; then smiled: "How're things in the big town, Willie?—in good old beery St. Looey."

"Okay," Yeager said, his voice husky from nervousness. "Better maybe than here."

At once Kalandyk appeared to tense, yet retained his thinly lethal smile. Then for the first time Yeager, still standing over him, saw him blink. It was a sudden hair-trigger closure of both eyes, shutterlike and instantaneous —three times. The three quick seizures seemed to stem from some blurred displeasure and left his face in a bland, vacant stare. "We try here to treat people right," he said gravely, turning from Yeager to Bea for confirmation.

"I've *told* him that, Bertie." Bea was grinding her teeth.

"Don't he believe it?"

"Sure, he does," jittery Bea said. "Right, Willie?"

For a strangely intended smile Yeager gave them his manic leer. "I *want* to," he said in an enigma, and returned and sat down at the table beside Darlene, who still ignored him.

Now Bismarck and old Jessie brought in two big platters of bacon, scrambled eggs, and hominy grits. Iris followed with buttered hot biscuits, and Bismarck soon returned with a huge pot of steaming coffee. Then, when everyone had sat down, he mumbled his customary short blessing over the food—as Kalandyk earnestly crossed himself. Soon they were all, eleven of them, eating. Through the window, beyond Bea's potted plants, they could see the slow, steady rain falling, and Yeager could barely hear the eerie church bells now; they seemed farther and farther away.

Kalandyk ate for a few moments in reflective silence, then casually announced: "I think I'll come and see the show tonight myself."

Bea's jaw dropped. She glanced fearfully at him. ". . . Bertie—oughtn't you let us kinda git the kinks out first?"

"Kinks—what kinks?" He looked at her, then down the table at Yeager. "I didn't know it still had any kinks." Then he smiled—"You got all this high-priced talent, here, from St. Looey. I've seen everybody in action but him, and you say he'll put Chester in the shade—so where's the kinks?" Then came the three sinister triggerlike blinks before he smiled again.

Iris, again down at the foot of the table, at the mention of Chester, was all ears.

Bea laughed nervously. "Maybe I didn't say it right, Bertie. There ain't no kinks, no—everything'll be all right. Only the second night oughta be a little better'n the first— ain't that right?"

"I don't see why. You say you're all set now, that you got again what you needed—ha, a pair of jacks?—and I know you wouldn't kid me." He gave his thin, arid laugh.

Bea's nostrils flared as she shot a glare down the table at Yeager, then blurted to Kalandyk—"You God-damn right I ain't kiddin' you, Bertie! You come right on to-night—you'll *see* I ain't!"

"Have you rehearsed with him yet?" Kalandyk glanced at Yeager before he looked at Bea again.

"No," she said. "But today, this afternoon, I'm having

'em all up in my room for a skull session."

"Donald, too?" Kalandyk grinned.

"Donald, too!" Bea gave a worried, false laugh.

"Ha, that should be quite a session."

Bea, chewing her food with heavy breathing, nodded vigorously for emphasis—"It *will* be."

"Should I hang around and see it?" Kalandyk, smiling whimsically, then turned from Bea to Donald—"Should I, Don?"

A stricken look came on Donald's face, but he fought to obliterate it. "I . . . I better let Bea handle that one, Bertie!" He laughed nervously.

Darlene, her face at last agonized, was squirming in her chair—she seemed struggling to keep silent. But soon she gave a crafty laugh. "No, no, Bertie," she said. "This is a closed affair this afternoon. Ha, ha, ha! But come back tonight and you'll see a *whing-ding* of a show!"

"You're damn right!" Yeager said, trembling with emotion. "One you'll never forget!"

Kalandyk sat up at this. He studied Yeager for a moment. But finally he smiled—"Good deal, Willie. Glad to hear you say it. Now you sound more like a real trouper."

"On second thought, though," Yeager said, again with his manic smile, "it may not be such a whing-ding show to *you*—because in your time you've seen a *lot* of blood."

Bea's mouth fell open. Her fork dropped to her plate.

". . . Blood? . . ." she breathed.

Darlene turned and gave Yeager a pained, puzzled look.

But Kalandyk seemed very interested—intrigued. Ignoring Yeager, he said to Darlene—"Sounds like you're gonna spring a *new* wrinkle on us. That right? Willie's brought some newfangled deal from St. Looey, eh? Well, we sure need some new ideas around here. Bea, that's what I've been harpin' on for months—and so have some of the customers. Whatever it is," he smiled, "you can bet some of them nuts up there tonight will love it. Right, Mack?"

"Right," Mack said.

Kalandyk grew reflective, pensive—"Jesus . . . *blood*. I don't get it . . . ." His gaze slowly drifted around the table again.

Darlene and Bea were still staring in bewilderment at Yeager. But Mack Thomas, frowning, spoke up: "Willie, here, is a real weird cat, if you ask me, Bertie," he warned. "I don't dig him, do you? Looka here, you better check this skull session out this afternoon like you started to. We can get all messed up, y'know, if this thing ain't right tonight—or if he don't know what he's doin', and gets rattled and runs amuck or somethin' . . . or goes off the deep end. . . . Damn! We could get the fuzz from *down-town*, man!"

Kalandyk had withdrawn into himself again and was meditative. "Bea's got everything under control," he finally said with his sinister coolness. "I'm not worried. Right, Bea?" Then came the level gaze.

Bea looked at him in return now. But instead of answering she delivered a fearful sigh.

"God, I hope so!" uneasy Mavis said.

But Cleo seemed only amused by the talk and, between coughs, laughed cynically.

Yeager masticated his food in silence.

Finally, when everyone had finished eating, Bea tried to recover some enthusiasm. She gave them a quick, harried smile—"Do you know what Bertie come by here for this mornin'? . . . Tell 'em Bertie."

Kalandyk only smiled.

"He's brought us a bonus!" Bea beamed. "That's what *he* calls it. *I* call it cash!"

Whereupon Kalandyk took an envelope containing money out of the inside pocket of his jacket and methodically passed out three hundred dollars each to Mavis, Cleo, Darlene, Mack, and Donald. "You're good folks," he said, "and doin' a good job. Keep it up."

Except for Darlene, the recipients, pleased beyond doubt, were generous with their thanks.

"I've meant to do it all along," Kalandyk said. "Just never got around to it. But when Mario, my dago brother in Naples, died last year, I knew I was goin' to get a little cash out of it eventually and said to myself, 'Don't forget

Bea's girls and boys, now.' I know my brother wouldn't like it, but he ain't around any more. He was a business man, religious and very respectable, in sweet old Napoli. Ha!—you didn't know I was a dago, did you? I sure am, and proud of it. Years ago I took the name I use now to out-fox the Feds, and just kept it. My real name's Alberto Mogadiscio—not Albert Kalandyk. Bea already knows this. Yeah, you folks treat me right, and I'll do the same with you. Dagoes and colored have a lot in common, y'know—both of us been kicked around a lot. So we oughta stick together."

"Now, ain't that the truth, Bertie!" Bea said.

Suddenly without warning Iris yelled up from the foot of the table at Kalandyk—*"Where's Chester!"*

Deathly silence fell.

Then Bea lunged up from the table and started for Iris —"I told you I was gonna whip your little ass!" she shrieked.

Bismarck jumped up and followed her—"Bea, don't you lay a hand on that child!" he said. "Leave her alone, now —she's just a baby and don't know when to talk and when to shut up, like a grown person would. Don't you touch her!"

Bea, her massive breasts heaving and falling, stood over petulant, cowering Iris. "Bismarck can't save you later on!" she screamed at her. "Git up from here and go to your room!"

Kalandyk's eyes were shuttering without letup now and his face was chalk-white. He took out a cigarette and nervously lit it.

Iris got up to go, yet stubbornly glared her anger up the table at him. Then she began wailing—"I want Chester! . . . I want Chester to come back! . . . when's *Chester* comin' back?" Big tears rolled off her cheeks and onto her cotton jumper. Now Bea grabbed her by the arm, dragged her to the door, and sent her sailing up the hall.

When Bea returned to the table, everyone, including Kalandyk, had gotten up to go. He bade them all a cold, formal good-bye, and, eyes still snapping, trailed Bea to the front and got his hat and coat from her. "I'll see you tonight," he said to her grimly, and left.

Meantime, Darlene, alarmed, had followed Yeager to his room. She was insistent. "What'n the world was you talkin' about? . . . *blood!*" she said, closing his door. "I spoke up and said what I did just to get 'em off of you. Then you start talkin' about blood. Oh, Christ, Willie! . . . But I don't get it, either! . . ."

". . . Rehearsal!" Yeager growled, turning from her, ignoring what she had said. "They *kept* talking about it —rehearsal! I don't have to go to any rehearsal—not any more." He paused, then spoke almost to himself, in a whisper—"I'm free of all that now. I've taken my stand . . ."

"Whatta you mean, you don't have to go?" She stepped in front of him. "You better start gettin' outa here, then. You can see Bea's scared to death that Bertie's on the verge of one of his wild, vicious spells. He was so damn mad and shook up about what Iris said, he was sick—you saw him turn white as a sheet and start blinkin' his eyes, didn't you? That's a bad sign. If you ain't goin' to leave here—and I can see you sure ain't—then you better come on up to Bea's room today like the rest of us. It'd damn near be suicide not to. You're the—"

"—What do you know about suicide?" he cut in, eyes burning. "Why do you bring that up? . . . Why, why?— tell me that!" He peered directly into her face.

She stared at him. "Willie, you have really gone stone crazy—honest to God, you have. What're you talkin' about! . . . I was just tryin' to tell you that if you ain't leavin' here, it ain't healthy for you to miss this skull session today—that's all! Then you come makin' a big issue outa suicide, from way out in left field—when there ain't nobody else thinkin' about it! Willie, what the hell's eatin' you! . . . You scare me to death!"

"I've taken my stand," he repeated, almost inaudibly.

"You talk about not goin' to Bea's room today, when *you're* the reason they're havin' the session. I keep tellin' you, Kalandyk ain't no man to fool with. If you *are* gonna join the show—and I'm ashamed to have to admit you are, no matter what you say—then it's a matter of your own neck to make that session. I've done every damn thing *I* could do to get you to leave this place, but you won't, so now I'm only tryin' to save your life. But you don't see it!" She was almost in tears.

All of a sudden he grabbed her and began shaking her violently. "Darlene!—*you're* the one who's got to leave here! Not me! Do you hear me?—you've got to leave, right away, before tonight! Don't be here for this show tonight!—I'm warning you! Tonight will be the last show! —there won't be any more after tonight! Ah, but what a show it will be! They will never have seen anything faintly resembling it—it will be the show you and Mack Thomas have feared all along, ever since I came here! There will be pandemonium! Don't be here!" His eyes had taken on a fanatic's glow. "Take my word for it, Darlene, and go to your room and get your coat and money and leave this house. I'll also give you what money I've got—I won't need it any more. Yes, yes, leave and don't come back!— for after tonight the Hippodrome will be *finished!*"

When he finally turned her loose, she stepped back from him stupefied. "Jesus God, Willie—what's up!" Her voice was full of fear. "What're you fixin' to do? Tell me! . . . Oh, please, tell me!"

"I'll tell you nothing!—no more than I have already.

What I have told you is to save you from getting arrested here tonight and doing time for being an inmate in such a place!"

"Willie! . . . Willie!—what're you sayin'? . . . what's gonna happen here tonight? I ain't goin' no place if you don't tell me what's up. Are you goin' to call the police? Is that it? . . . what? . . ."

"There'll be a *hundred* policemen here tonight!" he said wildly. "The place will be swarming with them! *I* won't be the one to call them, though! No . . . not I! Not . . ." His voice seemed to give out. He turned his back and went to the window. Outside, the rain had momentarily stopped —even the sun for a few minutes had broken through the ugly clouds. He stood looking down on the alley—muttering to himself. She called him once but if he heard he did not answer.

Soon she came over to him. She was trying to be calmer, more subdued now—"Willie, if I oughta be goin', then you should too. We oughta be goin' together . . . and keep together. But hear me good, now—we *are* goin' to be together—out there in the street, or here in this house. One or the other. Oh, Willie, I need you as much as you need me! . . . can't you see that? If you leave, I leave. But if you're gonna stay here, then I'm stayin'. That's the way it's gonna be. I'd swear it before my mother if I knowed who she was."

"*Oh!*" he said futilely, and went and sat down on the bed. He closed his eyes—"Leave this house, Darlene."

"Not by myself," she said quietly.

He opened his eyes and looked over at her before he spoke—"Do you realize the filthy, obscene life you've been living here? It's lower than an animal's—no beast would take part in one of these shows. Do you understand what you've been doing all the time you've been in this house? . . . up there in that awful room, two or three nights a week? . . . in front of all those horrible, savage, sick people? I went up there alone the other night, when the rest of you were out, and put on that one ghastly light in that room. Just *looking* at this foul, disgusting setting made me ill—and later made me vomit green bile. Your life here has turned your heart into a block of cement."

"My heart ain't half as hard as yours, Willie. It's terrible for you to say so."

"Are you still capable, though, of *any* sense of right and wrong? If you are, then you can't stay here any longer."

"You talk about knowin' right from wrong—you're stayin', ain't you?"

He took a deep breath. "Be patient—you'll understand better after tonight. But we weren't talking about me. Yet I haven't done the things you've done, have I?"

She came now and, sighing, stood over him. "Yes,

Willie—only worse . . . much worse. No, you ain't done exactly what I've done—*yet*. But you won't be so righteous after you leave Bea's room this afternoon—just wait. You'll find out what it's all about then, even though they'll only be goin' through the motions, not the real McCoy. Still, you'll be able to see, all right, what's goin' to happen tonight. You won't like it, either . . . *or will you.*"

He stared at the floor. ". . . I already know what's going to happen tonight," he said, emotion in his voice. "It's you who doesn't. Ah, it's my life . . . there will be the reckoning, the summing-up. I've been a moral man most of my life—in fact, I got caught in the meat grinder of my own corny morality. I'm finished now—finished. But you're not —I hope not. That's why you should leave—go somewhere and make a new beginning. In your case it's possible —in mine unthinkable." He stood up and turned his back on her again.

She spoke quietly, soberly. "I've told you, Willie, I won't go by myself. Let's don't rehash that. But if you'd only listen to reason, we could be gone from here in a half-hour. I've got over five hundred dollars now. Oh, Willie, we . . ."

He slowly shook his head. "It's no use. I want to thank you, though, for what you've tried to do for me since I came here. You've been the only friend I've had. Why did you want to help me? . . . why? Was it because you thought we were alike? . . . that we were both lost souls? Was it that? . . . we are, you know."

She looked away and did not answer.

He studied her for a moment—"I want to say good-bye, now."

". . . Good-bye?" Her eyes got big.

"Yes . . . Go, now, Darlene."

She stood watching him. "Poor, poor Willie," she said at last. "You been a mystery to me from the very beginnin'. But I can't help you—I can see that. You gotta look out for yourself now."

"Yes," he said.

"You better come on to Bea's room this afternoon, then. It's dangerous for you not to—whatever you're plannin'."

"Yes," he whispered. "I'll come . . . I must."

When she finally went to the door, he followed her.

"Good-bye," he said again.

She would not look at him, and left the room.

Chapter 10

LATER, he did not remember when darkness came. Yet
it enveloped and oppressed him now as he lay awake
on his bed in torment. He raised up on an elbow and peered
at his wristwatch, then remembered he could see nothing
in the blackness. He lay back down and shuddered yet once
more from the experience of the "session." They had all
gone up to Bea's room at three and were kept there until
after four-thirty, causing him now to wonder if the evening's events soon to come would not be anticlimactic
after all. He had returned to his room in a kind of mad-
dened daze, twitching and shuffling as if he had suffered
a paralytic stroke. And now with darkness had come the
slow steady rain again, its persistent dripping piercing the
walls of his room to create, instead of the room's height,
the sensation of dungeon dankness.

At the rehearsal Bea had been furious with him for his
clumsiness, ineptness, and had railed at him before them
all. But his mind was set and the ordeal had been necessary.
He had suffered her angry, humiliating crudities for his
own purposes—he would use her stage tonight to give
them their last show, the mounting of an apocalypse.
Nevertheless, thoughts of what soon impended sent him

159

quaking and trembling and he finally got up off the bed and put on the hated light. He saw now that it was already past six-thirty and he prepared to go to the kitchen for his dinner, knowing he would need the strength that food could give him—and the resolve.

In the kitchen he found old Jessie, Iris, and Mack Thomas. Iris stopped prattling the moment she saw him and went into a dour silence. Jessie, her lower lip full of snuff, told him to sit down at the table—where Mack already sat noisily eating a lamb chop. When he too had been served, he looked up to find Mack watching him. "Man, I wish I could figure you out," Mack said to him. "But I can't. I don't git this deal of Bea's at all, no foolin'. . . . Tell me, Willie, what *is* your story?"

Yeager began eating—fast, nervously, as if being pursued.

"Why, you ain't never been a swinger in your life, man," Mack said. "You're square as a box. You can see it all over you—it's plain as day—and just *bein'* here is about to kill you. I don't git it. In the first place, I can't figure out why you're here. Bea's got somethin' on you, ain't she?—huh?" Mack stopped chewing, leaned across the table, and fixed Yeager with a knowing stare—*"Ain't she?"*

Suddenly Yeager leered menacingly at him, and started to speak, but at last did not.

"Yeah, she's got you in a bind of some kind," Mack said—"And a bad one, at that. Cleo says the same thing— she thinks it's because you're in some kinda bad trouble or somethin'. Well, I got sense enough to know that if you are, you sure ain't gonna tell *me*. But I can tell *you* this— Watch your step and don't mess up this show tonight."

Yeager was strangely calm now; in his manner, almost cold. "I won't," he said, with his crazed smile. "The show will be *stupendous!*"

Mack finished eating and, shaking his head, left the kitchen.

In a few minutes Mavis, hurrying, officious, came in and said to Jessie—"Bea wants you to take one of those steaks outa the freezer. After the show Bertie might be hungry, and we sure don't want any trouble outa *him* tonight. Hear, Jessie?"

Jessie gave an exaggerated sigh and limped over toward the freezer.

After Mack Thomas's departure, Yeager was somehow able to eat more slowly. Now he had finished and was leaving the kitchen when Mavis said to him—"Willie, take my advice, and before we go up there tonight, throw down a couple of good stiff drinks. It'll help you get rid of some of your jitters." She became irritated—"You're makin' everybody else nervous! It's bad, you can see that. Donald's a nervous wreck already. We'll probably have the biggest mob in here tonight we've ever had in the whole history of the place. Bea's put the word out that our cast is up to strength again—not five any more, but six now—and this place'll be jammed, packed, and jumpin'. You heard Bertie say he's comin', and busy as he always is he don't hardly ever come to the shows. But I sure wish he wasn't comin' tonight—that's what's got everybody so nervous and upset too. And then *you* . . . Lord! Try and settle down some, if you can—and, as I said, take a couple of drinks just before we all meet up in the foyer. *This* sure ain't the night for somethin' to go wrong."

Yeager, nodding, finally sidled away from her and went to his room. He dropped down on the bed and, still whispering feverishly to himself, stared out the window again at the wet lights of the city. The sky was starless and black, and the dripping sounds outside persisted although a light wind had arisen. Activity throughout the house had already begun. He heard the little phonograph far up the hall playing gutty blues, and Iris capering up and down the hall squealing for Bismarck. Then Cleo laughed coarsely after yelling some remark at Mack Thomas, and Mavis ran back to borrow some eye make-up from Darlene. And soon Bismarck scurried by—lugging his whiskies and other bar supplies up to the foyer. Under the stark light Yeager looked at his watch again. It was already ten minutes past seven.

Then came a knock on his door. And Bea entered—
all dressed in red for the evening, her garish wig precariously in place, her rhinestone pumps glittering. She appeared clearly nervous and worried—disorganized. As he
sat on his bed, she came over and peered anxiously into
his face—"How'ya feel, Willie?" Her conciliating tone
surprised him, but he did not answer. Instead he gave his
leer again, and this time with the trace of a bitterly tri-
umphant smile. "I'm worried 'bout you," she said, "and
that evil bastard Mack Thomas just went to Bertie, who's
settin' up there right now in my room, and told him he was
scared about the show tonight, that it was a damn mistake
to have you in it, tonight or any other night, 'cause you
was a phony—a sleeper. Oh God, now Bertie's suspicious
—he's evil as hell tonight anyhow. Willie, *do* you wanta
put it off? . . . just yourself . . . 'til some other night, maybe? The others can still do the show . . . I told you before,
this ain't no laughin' or playin' matter—for you *or* me.
It's dangerous."

"You come begging now, eh?" Yeager said—again
there was the grimace, the malignant smile.

Bea flew into a rage. *"Yeah!* Yeah, I'm beggin'!—
because I'm scared! And if you hadda ounce of God-damn
sense, you'd be scared too!—for yourself! You don't know
Bert Kalandyk! . . . you may git to, though—soon! Why
d'you think I shanghaied you up here?—because you was

just the *perfect* one to take Chester's place?—huh? You
know damn well it wasn't!—I bet Donald's the first fag
you ever met in your life. No!—it was because I was desperate! That's what I keep tellin' Darlene when she says
I was nuts for bringin' you here. But what you-all don't
understand is that Kalandyk's had the heat on me for
weeks! . . . and finally told me I'd *better* find somebody.
I felt like tellin' him he oughta thought about that when
he up and made Chester do the disappearin' act so fast—
I didn't, of course. Still I could also see whut Bertie was
up against, too—it's hard here to just up and get rid of
somebody by firing 'em, and make it stick . . . I mean, get
away with it. Later on they can always talk, y'know. That
was Bertie's problem with Chester. But after Chester disappeared, the heat fell on me then—to get somebody to
take his place. And it's still on me. Why d'you think
Bertie's settin' up there in my room waitin'? He's protectin'
his investment, that's what he's doin'. He's makin' money
hand-over-fist in this place and wants to keep these peck
freaks comin' here at least three times a week. He wanted
to make it four—he's gotta shell out plenty to the police,
y'know—but my kids wouldn't go for that. I don't blame
'em—three nights is rough, as it is . . . you probably heard
Mack complainin'. But Bertie's gonna see to it when the
customers do come here, they get what they want—except
I draw the line on havin' children in the show, and told

him so. Some of these honkies, y'know, wanta see children
—the bastards! . . . Remember, I gotta child myself. But
Kalandyk's dead serious about pleasin' the customers, and
that way havin' the house full on every show night—an' I
can tell you he means business! So rather than see you go
up there tonight and make a fool outa yourself, and outa
me, like you done this afternoon—and outa Kalandyk!—
I'm beginnin' to think maybe you oughta wait 'til you
kinda get yourself together a little and calm down some.
Tonight you could just help out Bismarck on the bar again,
and then maybe next week sometime you might be in
better shape. Whatta you think about that? . . ."

At first Yeager was glowering, but now he gave his
slow cruel smile again—"But how would Mr. Kalandyk
take to that, I wonder?" He held his eyes on her.

Yet she managed to control herself, and gave a harried
sigh—"It'll be up to me, I guess, to handle him some way
or other, tonight. . . . I think maybe I can—'specially now
after what Mack's told him. Anyhow, it'll be better than
you goin' up there makin' a clown outa everybody, including Bertie. Lord!—you might not live to tell the story,
Willie. You better think damn careful what you're doin'."

He sighed. ". . . I have," he said.

Bea's mind was already elsewhere. "That little bitch
Darlene," she said angrily, "after all I've done for her,
came runnin' to me earlier this evenin', before Bertie

come, still beggin' me to let you off.... She acted like
she was scared as hell about somethin', too—but, oh,
Darlene's so simple and flighty. Hell, what's she care
'bout *my* neck while she's pleadin' for you! Even had the
gall—git this!—not only to ask me to let you off, but to
let you go on stayin' here.... said *she'd* pay your room
and board. How d'you like that? Darlene's awful dumb
'bout some things—you can see it . . . yeah, sometimes
she ain't got brain the first. Oh, Lord—she was all upset
and cryin' and goin' on. What's got into her?—what've
you done to her! I gave her holy hell and run her outa my
room. Bertie oughta heard her. God, is she addle-brained
—she's nuts!"

". . . Sure," he whispered—"sure . . . ." For a moment he
felt the sick ache of contrition.

"What're you gonna do, Willie? It's damn serious."

"What do you want me to do?"

Bea was in anguish. "Oh, Lord!—what do I want'ya to
do! . . . I want'ya to *use your head!* You're supposed to be
educated—well, use it!"

"Answer the question. What do you want me to do?"

She stared with open mouth, and at last exploded. "God-
damn your soul to hell! . . . you'll pay for this!—one way
or another! You can't bluff me! I'm givin' you a choice,
and if you go up there tonight and fuck up that show,
you'll never live to see mornin' . . . or if you do live, you'll

be behind bars 'til they fry your ass in the 'lectric chair!
That's a promise! Now, what do I tell Kalandyk?"

"Tell him to get there early and get a front seat!"

Shouting, cursing, she rushed out and slammed the door
almost off its hinges.

Yeager at once went to the closet and took out his robe.
Then he began to undress. But he was shaking so violently
he had to sit down on the bed for a moment and wait.
Finally, he had resumed undressing, when the terrifying
sound came—the doorbell up front was ringing for the
first time. He felt numb, wooden, until the aching fright
came over him once more and made breathing difficult.
Yet he slowly stripped naked, put on the robe, and lay
back across the bed to stare up at the light again.

Soon twice more the doorbell sounded, and when he
looked at his watch it was already 7:55. He knew now
that his former nemesis, Bea, worried, distraught, rushing
about—but dressed to kill, her awkward red wig flowing,
the costume jewelry clattering—was up at the front door
greeting the early guests and collecting their ten-dollar
admissions. In his mind he could also see old Bismarck
stationed behind the bar, calmly, discreetly, awaiting the
crush of patrons he must serve before the next hour had
passed. Suddenly he thought of Darlene and longed to
rush across the hall, get down on his knees even, if necessary, and thank her—thank her for what she had tried,

though failed, to do for him . . . and, of all people, it had been Bea who was the callous witness. He also longed, for the last time, to try to persuade Darlene to leave this house in these her final minutes of choice, but knew she would only revile him, so he did not move from the bed.

The doorbell rang twice more in quick succession. He closed his eyes against the brazen light and tried to slow the pounding at his temples, striving to survive the next hour of waiting before the summons would come. Soon the doorbell was ringing repeatedly, and already he could hear the familiar, growing noise of talk and hilarity up front in the foyer. The glaring light above him now became unbearable and he got up and flicked off the wall switch. Then he sat in the dark by the window, gazing down once more on the lighted alley which was still a bog of mud although the rain had stopped, and at the lighted back stairs of the building next door. In each instance when it seemed that time had stopped, the doorbell would ring again and the clamor up front increase. But again he would lapse into a feeling of the complete cessation of time, until the doorbell began ringing every minute and the boisterous noise at last became a din. Now he tried to read his wristwatch, but again in the darkness failed. Yet he was certain it was past 8:30 and his heart began such a violent, furious pounding it seemed his chest would burst. Once more he tried to pray, but it was no use.

He was conscious of only one thing now—that he was experiencing the preparing power of chaos; that his suffering was a necessary prelude to the reestablishment of something even he could not too clearly define; that out of the loathsome emptiness of his life would now be forged something like a new essence, a sort of state of non-being, through the choice that he now freely made. Yet there was a grain of self-mockery in all this, he knew; for, throughout his life, every time he had dared look into himself, *inside* himself, he had there seen it all so vividly—as if a huge mountain loomed before him—i.e. *nothing*. He had, in fact, been able to evolve this "nothing" into a heady, if ponderous, concept; the concept of Nothingness—whose central theme was only that existence is detestable. Yet it was a concept the heart could feel. Accordingly, what he was now about to do had unfolded within the silence of the heart. It, therefore, had a truth of its own. So tonight would merely gain the solution to the absurd—that was all. The dark of his room now felt to him all-enveloping. At the window he suddenly aroused himself. *"I take my stand!"* he said, shivering with emotion—and at long last he wept.

Finally, far out across the dark horizon he saw the lights of a jetliner—a DC-9, as best he could identify it— making its slow descent toward the airport just outside the city. He had an inspiration. He would force his eyes to stay on these moving lights until they were out of view, and thus try to break his seige of pain and fright. The DC-9's air speed was slow now, and its blinking lights seemed almost suspended; its progress was smooth, gentle, effortless, in the approach to the far-off runway. But gradually getting lower, the lights became more distant, and dimmer. They seemed somehow slowly fading as they sank lower and lower toward the rim of city lights. Although he knew the sight could not last much longer, his eyes clung to it desperately, recklessly, and even when it finally sank from view, he went on staring at the black spot where it had disappeared.

Now as he looked away he realized the noise up in the foyer had changed; it had peaked—become excited, jaded, hoarse; then it began to stir, to move, and with a shock of dread he knew the reason—at last the double doors of the arena had been thrown wide. He could sense the crush of the crowd in motion, shoving, surging forward. He jumped up and flicked on the light, trying to control his panic, and stood trembling in the middle of the floor—waiting. While naked except for the robe, he still could not feel the damp chill of the room, though almost five minutes passed. Then suddenly he heard Bea's voice. It was desperate, fierce, yet croaky from over-use, as she came down the hall summoning her troupe. *"Okay, you-all!"* she cried. *"Let's go!"*

He took two steps backward—toward the dresser—but hesitated when his heart seemed to founder. Finally, he turned, went to the dresser, and took the gleaming dagger-knife from under the newspaper liner of the middle drawer. For an instant he viewed it curiously, before he slipped it in the right-hand pocket of his robe and stood waiting again. The hollow pounding in his chest produced a dead thudding in the eardrums, and for a moment he was dizzy.

Bea banged on Mavis's door first, then on Mack Thomas's. *"Okay, okay!"* she cried hoarsely. "Look alive, now, you-all! Let's go! They're expectin' big things from us up there!—Oh, Lord, how I hope we don't disappoint 'em. . . . Nobody but a fortuneteller, though, could tell how this thing's comin' out tonight. But with what I been through, and my sky-high blood pressure and bad heart, I'll be lucky to last *out* the night. And you-all be quick and alert, now, to cover up for that damn Willie's fuck-ups. That man's gotta be the saddest sack in the history of the world—and a fool!"

Mack Thomas came out of his room grouching—"He ain't the only fool in this place."

"Shut up, Mack," Bea said, and continued. "We got the biggest crowd in here of all time! You couldn't git another peckerwood in up there with a shoehorn! Lord, the fire marshall would pitch a bitch if he could see this place tonight! Poor Bismarck's a wreck. Come on, now, you-all!"

Yeager heard her coming nearer—*"Show time! . . .* Darlene, come outa there!" she called in a rasping, depleted
voice. He drew the belt of his robe tighter, re-tied it, and
stepped close to his door—the brown color of his face had
turned ashen, his lips blue-black and cold. He waited.

Across the hall Bea was pounding on Darlene's door
now. And in the next instant come the knock on his own.
He opened the door at once, but, stepping out into the
hall, he seemed to stumble—he was not sure. There had
been no object in his path but, frowning, he turned around
and looked down as if he had been tripped. It was only
then he realized his legs had gone rubbery again, and now
he summoned every reserve of strength he had to walk
at all.

Darlene came out of her room but would not look at
him. Both of them followed Bea up the hall, until, about
halfway, Darlene suddenly stopped, here eyes wide with
wonder, fear, and stared at him as if he were a ghost. She
seemed once more about to speak, to plead with him, but
instead, sighing, resumed walking. They soon joined the
others who had already emerged from their rooms. When
they had all reached the foyer, Bea whispered loudly—
"Line up, kids! . . . line up!" But she was so nervous and
scared she was inefficient—"Line up over *here!* Hurry!
Okay, let's give 'em a show tonight that'll curl their
straight hair—that they'll never forget as long as they're

honkies! . . . *Shhhhh!* . . . Come *on,* you-all—line up!"
Cleo, observing Bea, laughed. And now they could hear
the excited buzz of the great crowd inside the arena. "You-
all better snap out of it," Bea said—"Bertie's here!" Cleo
laughed again.

They all soon formed the line. Bismarck, doddering and
sweaty, was already dismantling the bar. He glanced at
Yeager, then discreetly turned his back. For Donald the
occasion appeared extra-special—his copper-colored natural was coiffed unusually high on his head tonight,
daringly, dramatically, and his eyes were wide with excitement. But Mack Thomas seemed stoical again now.
Yeager, though feeling faint, once more tried to catch
Darlene's cold stare, but could not. Finally she glanced in
his direction and appeared defeated, resigned—prepared
for whatever was to come.

All the troupe were in their robes—the men barefoot.
Cleo, at the moment not coughing, seemed serious now,
serene, and wore her delicate earrings that brought to mind
staid heirlooms. Mavis, in her usual place at the head of
the line, laughed and called over to the bar—"Hey, Bismarck! How about a glass of champagne?" Bismarck
grinned—"Sure, baby. I'll ice a bottle just for you, and it'll
be ready right after the show. You'll be my guest." Mack
Thomas's eyes got big; right away he said—"Man, you
got an idea there!" He turned to the others—"How 'bout

that, you-all? Let's pitch in and pop some champagne after the show. Ha! We'll toast this clown Willie's first night —if we git through it."

In the hall Kalandyk had just stepped from Bea's room. Dignified, unobtrusive, almost shy, he came up into the foyer—wearing an impeccable black suit and pearl grey tie. Having heard Mack, he said to them—"No, we'll do it this way—if you go in there and put on the show of your life tonight, there'll be a *case* of champagne for you afterwards—on the house."

"Hey, now!" cried Mack—"You gotta deal, Bertie!"

Kalandyk left at once and went into the arena.

Bea, looking harried, exhausted, still exhorted them— "Okay, let's go in there and wow 'em and git that champagne, then. And look *happy,* will'ya? Don't forget what I've told you agin and agin—they always expect us to be happy! Don't ask me why—I'll be God-damned if I know. But they do. We ain't got a pot nor a window, but we're supposed to be happy!" She was trying for levity, but the troupe only grinned—they too seemed anxious, tense, now. Bea looked down the line—after Mavis, stood Donald, then Cleo, Yeager, Darlene, and finally Mack Thomas. Bea now went back to bring up the rear. ". . . *All set?*" she called—"Okay, then, let's go." Mavis bravely stepped off and led the file into the arena.

Yeager's walk had degenerated into a desperate shuffle.

But strangely once he entered the room, the weakness seemed to leave his legs. Though in a daze, he tried to stand straighter, and momentarily his trembling ceased. Yet he feared for his faculties, and sought to clear his mind in order to act.

As they all entered, a hush fell on the crowd. When Bea, the last to come, closed the double doors and threw the bolt in the lock into place, the great room was in semidarkness—an ominous gloaming. The only light was the single bulb, with shade, suspended directly over the cot. The cot now had a starched white sheet on its mattress and a stack of fresh hand towels underneath on the floor. Every seat up in every tier was occupied. Standees were packed around the walls at every unobstructed point and also jammed just inside the double doors where the cot could be seen only with difficulty. Kalandyk, his cold eyes already shuttering, also stood against the wall on the near, the foyer, side of the room—but at a spot he had chosen from which he could see everything.

Mavis led the single file through the crush of heavy-breathing spectators to the cot in the well of the arena, then around it once. When they had finally halted they stood forming a rough circle around the cot and its dangling light. Then, with smiles of mechanical radiance, they all turned around, faced their respective parts of the circular audience, and bowed to the eager applause. Suddenly

Yeager began trembling again and his knees went limp. His mouth also now moved incessantly as if in some silent, futile prayer that had once more brought spittle to his lips.

Finally, Bea stepped to a spot inside her circle of performers and beside the cot under the light, a brilliant smile wreathing her face, and waited for the applause to stop. Then she began to speak—"*Good evenin'*, Ladies and Gentlemen! *Welcome!* . . . again welcome! We all sure do wanta thank you for this wonderful, beautiful greetin' you just gave us! . . . and for comin' out in droves like this— Lord, this place is bustin' at the seams tonight, ain't it? . . . This has gotta be the biggest crowd we *ever* had! And you got an entertainin' evenin' ahead of you, too, let me tell you—we have finally seen to *that*, all right. Now, mosta you have been here before, so you know all my entertainers. That is, except one! We gotta new addition to our group! *Willie Carter!*—from St. Louis!" Beaming, from fear laughing distractedly, she stepped back from the cot, out of the cone of light, and called over to Yeager—"Step up here, Willie, and take a bow!"

Yeager, shaking violently now, his hands in both pockets of his robe, stepped to the cot in the funnel of light. The spontaneity of the applause indicated he had been long awaited. He bowed feebly once, then, ignoring Bea, cleared his throat to speak. She gasped. But before he spoke he withdrew both hands from the pockets of the robe and all could see that his right hand gripped a knife. The audience gasped now. Then in a clear, though dry, high-pitched voice, he addressed them—"I take my stand! . . . I appear before you tonight in order that you may witness my victory!" Then gripping the knife like a dagger, while distending his breast as the target, he raised the knife high above his head—to drive it into his heart. For a moment he held it there—poised. Then he faltered. The crowd gasped again—and sat paralyzed. Still he held the knife aloft—though quaking now. The room was petrified. Strangely now he grunted, and, as if to screw up his cour-age, gave a frantic little lurch, as though trying to raise the knife higher, and yet higher, for the act. Finally, he let it clatter to the floor. He stood there looking blank, then desperate, helpless, his spittled lips apart. At last he slumped to his knees—trembling, laughing, crying. "I couldn't do it!" he whimpered to them all—"I couldn't! . . . *Oh, God, I couldn't do it!*" he cried aloud in a great wail, and dove his face into his hands—as Darlene screamed, then became hysterical.

Bea, her mouth hanging open, was paralyzed—im-mobile.

Suddenly Donald, his silk cerise robe flying, rushed for-ward. He stood quivering over Yeager, who, sniveling, still knelt, and with the tips of his dainty fingers just touched the top of Yeager's head—yet as if somehow solemnly annointing him. Then after a gazelle's high, wild leap of ecstacy, he did an almost perfect pirouette, landing exactly where he had stood, and nimbly, gracefully, bent and kissed the back of Yeager's head—as Yeager's suddenly-awakening, excited eyes began to gleam like diamonds. Donald now reached down and urged him to his feet, then made a sweeping, satyrlike bow to him before, right hand thrown wide, offering him to the crowd for their approval. The crowd went wild. A stormy ovation ensued. Great outbursts of shouts and applause rocked the room. The place was in a frenzy.

Kalandyk, his face livid, rushed out in front of the audience frantically waving his arms—"*Shhhhh! Shhhhh! Shhhhh!*" he cried. But ecstatic delirium swept the room for another full minute before finally the noise began to subside, and at last slowly ceased. Meanwhile, Donald had retrieved the knife off the floor and now led Yeager, who seemed rapturous, transfigured, back out of the light to his original place in the circle. Darlene sobbed softly.

"*Bea! Bea!*" Kalandyk yelled. "Get on with it!—get on with the show! God-damn it, go ahead! . . . They're makin' too much noise!"

Dazed Bea at last came forward once more, but with a face stricken dumb. The moment she stepped into the light, wild applause erupted all over again. Though unsteadily, she held up both hands now until she could be heard, and finally her smile returned. *"Whew!"* she said to them, breathing heavily—"Y'see, Ladies and Gentlemen, whut you're in for tonight, don't you? Lord, it's almost too much even for an old vet like me. Whew! But I'll have to ask you not to clap no more, or holler. We got a rule against that here, y'know. . . . I don't have to tell you, the noise could bring us trouble. Say, whut's got into you-all tonight, huh? Ha! ha! ha!—I never heard you carry on like this before! We like it, but it's dangerous. . . . So no more applause, please, folks!" Her eye now spotted straw-haired Marty, boisterous and irrepressible as ever, up in the third tier of seats. "You, too, Marty," she grinned. "Cool it a little, will'ya?"

"Sure, sure, sweetheart!" Marty laughing, yelled down —"Anything you say! Just git this damn show on the road!" He was salivating.

"Right!" Bea said. "Now, let's get on with it!—whatta'ya say? So we're gonna start off with our little act that's always such a crowd-pleaser—called 'My Little Chickadee.' You remember. It starts out with a solo act by cute little Mavis, here, who will then be joined by that rampagin' billy goat you-all love so—Mack Thomas! *Oooooh!* —let's get with it, then! . . . *Show time!"*

Mavis stepped forward into the funnel of light, slowly, teasingly, shimmied out of her robe, and the show was on.

Chapter 11

H OURS later, when the crowd had all gone, the wild champagne party in Bea's room lasted from midnight until daybreak. There was total elation. Triumph had emerged from almost certain disaster. Now there was only relieved delight and excitement—the hilarity of success. The troupe had bathed, donned relaxing sweaters and slacks, and gathered in Bea's room around the case of iced champagne Kalandyk had provided, while he quietly ate his steak off her dresser top and gave them all reserved, pixyish smiles. Then he left, and the festivities began in earnest.

"Oh, God, *that's that!*" Bea, already half drunk, breathed in deliverance. "Bertie sure was spoilin' for trouble tonight, wasn't he? Whew! Lord, was he evil! He'da been hard to handle if things hadn't turned out right—I was scared shitless and ain't ashamed to admit it. But Willie, here, come through like a champion, didn't he? Lord God! —was that boy groovey! Who'da thought it! *Now* what you got to say, Mack Thomas? Haw, haw!"

"Yeah, the cat was terrific!" Mack said. *"Terrific!"*

Yeager, seated over in the corner with Mavis, a glass of champagne in his hand, smiled at the floor—and across the room Donald beamed.

"He sure was!" Mavis cried, laughing. She kissed him— "Welcome to the club, Willie, baby!"

"The cat's a star overnight," Mack said. "Even there at the last you couldn't hardly stop him. An iron man! You know who's glad, too, don't you? *Me*. He can take some of this weight offa *me*. I told you I been ruinin' my health in this pad. Yeah, Willie's whut you call *versatile*. Right, Donald?"

Donald squealed. "Oh, shut up, Mack!"

"He had them pecks in the palm of his hand from the word go," Mack said—"'specially when he pulled that fake suicide stunt with the knife. Now, *that* floored everybody—even Darlene—'cause he made it so real! Jesus!— for a minute there my mouth was open and I couldn't git it shut. It was enough to make your blood run cold. Then foxy old Donald got in the act—couldn't hardly wait for his turn, ha! Yeah, Willy made history—he turned Mavis on too, didn't he?"

"Right, Mack!—right!" Mavis was ecstatic, then turned to Yeager. "Willie, baby, you was beautiful—*beautiful!*" she said, kissing him on the ear. He smiled at her.

Darlene, across the room near Donald, and drinking heavily, sat glowering disgustedly at Yeager. Finally, she got up and staggered out of the room.

Old Bismarck, sitting near the door, yawned now and grinned—"I ain't high, like the rest of you-all are, but I'm tired and goin' to bed too." He soon got up and followed Darlene.

Suddenly Yeager, eyes glowing, spun around to Mavis. "Where's the *music?*" he said excitedly, impatiently— "You said you were going to get your phonograph!"

"Okay, sweetie—right now." Mavis jumped up and went to her room and soon brought back the portable phonograph he had been hearing for days from afar. The eight records she also brought were all either blues or hot jazz.

He took the records from her quickly and examined the label of each. He seemed disappointed. "I thought maybe you might have a waltz here too," he said.

"A *waltz!*" Mavis threw back her head in a wild, ringing laugh. "Willie, what'n the hell are you talking about?—people don't waltz any more! I don't even know how, very well—do you?"

"Sure!—of course I do."

Jubilant Bea, though in all the noise too far away to hear their conversation, laughed and yelled at them— "*Say,* whut's goin' on over there, you two? You-all come outa that corner and join the party. The show's over, y'know! Haw!"

"Bea!" Mavis cried, "Willie wants to *waltz!*"

"Willie's nutty as a fruit cake!" Bea said. "Oh, but is he groovey!—ha, *right,* Mavis? No, they didn't even waltz in my day—my God."

Yeager reached and tossed off his champagne and, smiling again, eyes afire, handed the glass to Mavis for a refill. "The waltz is a wonderful dance!" he suddenly cried—"Wonderful! . . . it's really a sort of fantasy. It *is* a fantasy! . . . yes, a vision!" The others stopped talking and turned around to listen. "Didn't you ever try it?" he said eagerly—"Oh, you can get so lost, so carried away, in a beautiful, spinning, swirling waltz!" He stood up and began humming and sweeping both arms from side to side in three-quarter time.

"Now the cat's actin' like Donald," Mack Thomas said. "It's catchin'!"

Yeager seemed not to hear. "Like this—*see?*" he said, and, closing his eyes, humming a waltz, he started dancing around alone on Bea's wall-to-wall carpet. "It makes everything a fantasy, sort of, you see!" he cried—"Like a vision! . . ."

Meanwhile, Mavis had put on one of the records. As soon as the rough, raucous music began, Yeager stopped dancing, his face again showing disappointment. "That's vulgar!" he said—"Don't you see what I mean? . . . it's lowdown! A waltz is not!"

"You damn right it's lowdown!" drunken Mack Thomas guffawed—"that's whut's good about it! Only it ain't lowdown *enough*—put on some of that old time huckle-buck, Mavis!"

Yeager tried to speak again, but, resuming their loud, gleeful antics, the others ignored him. When the first record had played through, Mavis put on another, also raucous, honoring Mack's request. The moment the music started, Yeager jumped up, grabbed her, and nonetheless began trying to waltz. The others howled, bawled, with laughter. Mavis, herself soon crying from laughing, attempted to wriggle free. "Willie!—Willie! This is huckle-buck music!—this ain't no waltz! My God!—what're you tryin' to do? You heard Bea say the show's over! Ha! ha! ha!" Still another shout of laughter went up from them. But Yeager, eyes closed again, a seraphic smile on his face, clutched her to him and continued trying to waltz, although the music was loud and grating and had a synco-pated beat. "Isn't waltzing glorious, dizzying? . . ." he turned and cried to them all. He was almost in tears, hysterical—"You see, don't you? It's not vulgar! . . . It's not at all!" They were awed now, and watched him curi-ously. "Vulgar . . . no," he reflected aloud, then said to them over Mavis's shoulder—"But even if it is, I have read that we can win redemption through vulgarity, through degra-dation. Through *degradation*—yes! Do . . . do you believe that? . . . do you really think there's . . . there's redemp-tion—for anyone, *ever?* It may be true . . . after all. If so, I am redeemed, eh? . . . for I have experienced degradation tonight. I have seen the sick evil, the sinful fury of hell itself, in the human soul—my own included!—here to-night. Hence I am degraded—below any animal that ever lived. Ah, but we're *all* capable! Aren't we therefore also capable—worthy!—of redemption? I ask you! . . . I ask you. . . ." In his abstraction, he had almost stopped danc-ing and was largely leaning on Mavis's shoulder.

"Turn me *loose,* Willie!" Mavis cried, and began play-fully pummeling him on the chest. At last he let her go and she laughed in his face, then kissed him again. "Willie, you excite me," she whispered. "Couldn't you tell it in the show?" She grew meditative—"Come on, let's have some more champagne. Then I'll dance with you again."

He seemed somehow elated, and beamed at her. And after another glass of champagne, they waltzed again to more hucklebuck music. Then he suddenly left her and went over and asked Bea to waltz. Bea doubled up laugh-ing, but got up, daintily smoothed down her house dress, and they began. But to the harsh, rhythmic, staccato music playing they could only stumble about. Yet Bea was un-caring. "Willie," she said, happy and perspiring, "you're gonna be with us now, all right! Oh, boy!—didn't it work out wonderful after all! Was you a *sensation!* Bertie don't let on—that's his way—but he's tickled pink. . . . Told me for at least one night a week now we might even raise our prices—to *fifteen dollars!* Yeah! How'dya like that?—we'll all git our cut, of course. Oh, Willie!— all because of you. And I had about give up, think of it!

Lord, was I lucky!" Then she turned to them all and let out a half-drunken cry—"*Whooop-e-e-e-e!* . . . Willie's our boy!"

"Oh, Bea, baby!" Donald, also full of champagne, caroled from across the room—"You're gonna bust a gut if you ain't careful!" Then he jumped up and came toward them as they danced in the middle of the room. "May I cut in?" he laughed—"Bea, you go sit down and rest awhile."

Bea hollered with laughter—"Didn't you hear me tell Mavis a minute ago the show's over!" She doubled up again. But then she disengaged herself from Yeager and obligingly stepped back. Yeager, standing alone now, snarled at Donald—"You get away from me!" he quivered. Donald looked surprised, and hurt; he dropped his hands, stared, and soon went back and sat down dejectedly. Yeager returned to Mavis.

But soon they were all drinking, dancing, and making a storm of noise again. Cleo, who, as she drank champagne, had also been smoking a marijuana cigarette, got up and, slightly staggering, asked Mack Thomas to waltz with her. Mack gave her a sneering laugh, then jumped up, seized her roughly, and instead began doing a breakneck Watusi. "Here's your fuckin' waltz!" he shouted, panting, as he wildly gyrated his hips and shoulders. The moment Yeager saw them he shrieked— "*That's vulgar!*" He spun around to Mavis—"Stop that music! Stop it, Mavis!" Mavis gaped at him but soon turned the phonograph off. The others stood looking in both curious wonder and irritation. Then he held up both hands for silence, closed his eyes again, and began humming, at first softly, then louder—the Blue Danube Waltz. Soon, his face mesmerized, he began sweeping his arms once more and swaying in three-quarter time. "*Now!*" he cried—"Now you can waltz! Come on! . . . Taaah-taah-taah, *TA*! ta-ta, ta-ta . . . Taaah-taah-taah, *TA*! ta-ta, ta-ta . . . Taaah-taah-taah, *TA*! ta-ta, ta-ta . . . Come on, come on!—dance, *dance,* won't you!" He reached and took Cleo in his arms, and they danced gracefully, beautifully, in great dipping swoops, as he hummed for them all to hear—"Taaah-taah-taah, *TA*! ta-ta, ta-ta!" Although slightly taller than he, Cleo put her head on his shoulder and closed her eyes. Mack stared at them for a moment, then pulled Mavis to him and also began waltzing. And soon Donald and Bea were on their feet and dancing to Yeager's loud, ecstatic humming. Now they were all waltzing—feverishly, wildly, and soon frenziedly. This continued for almost five minutes. Finally Yeager, out of breath, beads of perspiration on his forehead, tired. He stopped humming. And soon they all slowly, reluctantly, stopped dancing—like a clock's alarm running down—and, silent, subdued, found seats and sat down. But suddenly Yeager seemed even more agitated

—excited. There was a manic blaze in his eyes as he turned to them all once more—"Do you see? . . . I believe it *is* a dream! . . . only a dream, maybe! . . . yes! Being here is just a dream! . . . so what need is there for redemption? Again, I ask you . . . what? . . ."

There was a slight noise out in the hall. Then Darlene reappeared in the doorway. She was in her robe again, and, weaving on the threshold, held a tall whiskey highball in her left hand. Now, looking at Yeager, she slowly, menacingly, put her right hand in her robe pocket. Mack Thomas, watching her, jumped up. "You better git outa here, Willie—quick," he whispered to Yeager. "Looks like she's gunnin' for you—I think she's got her little Beretta automatic." Yeager did not move, and when Darlene, her hand still in her pocket, came over and stood in front of him, everyone got quiet.

Finally Bea, alarmed, spoke up. "Now, now, Darlene— don't you start any rough stuff in my house! Here, gimme that gun! . . . You hear, Darlene! . . ." She stood up.

Darlene, unsteady, still stood over Yeager—glaring at him as she muttered something inaudible and occasionally sipped the drink.

Meanwhile, Mack Thomas was stealing up behind her. Suddenly he lunged, grabbed both her arms—the drink flying—and pinned them to her side. She began cursing and screaming and wrestling him savagely. He held her.

"Turn loose of that rusty little thing, Darlene," he said
—"We don't want no shootin' in here. Turn loose, now,
and I'll let you go." Still she fought him. Finally he
seized her wrist that was in the pocket, applied cruel
pressure, and jerked out her empty hand. He reached in
the pocket then and, instead of a gun, brought out her
little Bible.

"Oh, Lord," Bea breathed in relief. "Ha, the Good Book.
Darlene, you're drunk." Then Bea stooped to pick up the
scattered ice cubes off her carpet, as Mack tossed the Bible
on her bed.

Darlene began screaming at Yeager. "You rotten, filthy
freak, you!—you sanctimonious son of a bitch! . . . I was
gonna throw it in your *face!*" She sat down on Bea's bed
and swiping the Bible aside, began crying. And the more
Cleo and Mavis, both bewildered, tried to console her, the
more she sobbed. Yeager viewed her impassively, and
merely poured himself another glass of champagne. Mavis
started the phonograph again now and soon all, except
Darlene, sat clapping to the beat of the hot jazz.

Then as the second record was playing, tipsy Bea went
over and asked Mavis to dance. "Now, look out, Bea!"
Mavis laughed in warning—"Don't let that champagne
go to your head." Bea first frowned, then grinned—"You
fine little bitch, you. I'm gonna fire you one of these
days if you ain't careful." "Ha," Mavis sneered, "that's

what you think." Bea's eyes opened—"Whut you mean?" Mavis slightly raised her chin—"I just mean you can't fire me, that's all." "Yeah . . . yeah," Bea said reflectively, "I have figured that, y'know—I figured you'd be screwin' that dago before long. Yeah, I can see it now—in Bertie's shifty eyes. Well, just put this down in your little black notebook—you'll never take your social security or git to be an old woman. . . . They'll find you some cold winter day in a ditch, froze stiff as a board, with a 38 slug behind the ear. You mark my words." Audibly sucking her teeth now, she staggered away from Mavis.

Meanwhile the hilarity went on without letup. And soon Yeager wanted them all to waltz again. But they laughed and ignored him. Finally he went over to Darlene, still seated on Bea's bed, and tried to get her to waltz with him. Although she had stopped crying, she sipped a glass of champagne mournfully. "Come on, Darlene," he said, his eager voice pitched strangely, nervously, high—"Let's waltz! Come *on!*" he pleaded. She flatly refused, and curled her lip angrily. "You are the lowest dog I ever run into," she said—"But didn't I predict it? I sure did! I had a funny feelin' all along about you—and told you so, even when you was doin' all that talkin' about the Bible, and about your damn morals, *and mine!*"

His face sobered for a moment, but as he sat down beside her now he gave a short, dry, crazy laugh. "*Ha, ha!*

You're so sure about everything," he said, "but after tonight what can we ever be sure about? What? How do we know anything? As I said while you were out, what if all this is just a dream, a bad dream? . . . just like my life—and yours. I didn't realize this might, or could, be true until tonight—up there in that roomful of sordid whites. It was a revelation—like being caught in the middle of an earthquake. I was in something like a coma. I was also mad, possessed—my weeks of ordeal had at last destroyed, obliterated me."

"Shit," Darlene said.

"No, no—the mind can take only so much. It's not as strong as you may think—under enough weight, it will give way. Of course, now I'm in ruins. I will be for the rest of my life—however long or short that may be. So in the future, I can only be sure of *nothing.*"

"Willie, all you do is make a lotta excuses for yourself —one right after another! . . . and talk all that high falutin' crap and theories and religious stuff about things nobody listenin' to you understands anyhow, includin' yourself. All the time I thought you was crazy, just crazy, but I was wrong. You're *phony,* Willie . . . that's it—phony as a three-dollar bill!"

He studied her, then for a moment stared at the floor. "I've considered that," he nodded. "I know myself better than you think. And maybe I should confess the truth of what you say—I probably won't, but maybe I should. Yet a good case can be made for the phony life, you know. A long, long time ago, when I was in the university—I mentioned that to you—a professor named Bjorncrantz told us some things I didn't think much about at the time. Ah, but I have since. He asked us to consider the possibility that reality consists merely of particles of matter moving in space and time according to laws of necessity. That matter is the ultimate reality. That our sense organs are transformers, not revealers. That man does not have a free will. That all human action is motivated by complete selfishness. And that religion is a pill one had best swallow quickly without chewing. Ha, old Bjorncrantz, in just that one afternoon, gave us something to think about for the rest of our lives, didn't he? I must say, too, that as time has gone on, the impression on me of what he said that day has become almost indelible. It has often made me ask myself, what *can* I be sure about?" In his sudden intensity Yeager almost stood up from the bed. "Maybe, then, Darlene, we worry needlessly! Things could be the very opposite of what they seem. This . . . this could be—maybe is—a *good* house!"

Darlene gasped; her hand went to her mouth.

His eyes were glowing again. "Yes! . . ." he said, "maybe all that I've seen, and been through, here is just a vision, a fantasy! It could be, you know—even my whole sorry

life, and yours too, could be a damned fantasy, or dream
... a confused, absurd dream! ... addling, dizzying ...
and maybe gotten rid of merely by going around and
around in a beautiful dance—yes, in a beautiful, lilting
waltz! Don't you see, Darlene? Yes! ... yes—maybe the
Hippodrome is really the *house of God!*"

"*Oh!*" Then Darlene sat petrified, shocked. She would
not look at him.

At that moment pretty Mavis, giddy from much champagne, came up, threw her arms around his neck, and
kissed him hungrily, passionately. "Come on, Willie," she
said—"let's dance!" As she led him away his eyes were
still glowing. Head down, Darlene left.

When dawn came at last and the party had ended,
Yeager, still unsurfeited, went with Mavis to her room
and slept with her.

Chapter 12

LATER that day, around noon, it resumed raining, and about one o'clock the rain turned to large hail. The hail woke Yeager. His head was splitting from the champagne. Soon he got up and left Mavis's room and went to his own. After awhile he dragged himself back to the kitchen for aspirin and black coffee. Old Jessie, drooling snuff, was grumbling about Darlene—"You can't tell that crazy gal nothin'; she's gotta head like a rock. You see whut it's doin' out there—all that rain and hail; well, whut's she do? ... why, she goes outa here with some little old thin shoes on like she'd be wearin' on the prettiest day in June. I tried to tell her to put her boots on, but she rushes outa here almost like she was deaf; you watch, she'll be wet up to her knees when she comes back. I told her this is pneumonia weather, but I might as well been talkin' to a rock. Darlene's nuts!" He wanted to stuff his fingers in his ears to shut out her drivel, but he only sat there holding his head and sipping the coffee, saying nothing.

It was raining steadily again when he returned to his room, and he stood at the window gazing down on the drab, wet, familiar scene. He had lost all sense of time, of days, and when painfully he tallied up the days and nights and realized it was now Monday afternoon, the fact so startled him that he wondered if he was right. His head still throbbed and he sat down on the bed, yet could think very little. He considered this merciful—it would, for a time at least, keep his febrile mind away from himself. Even at two o'clock the house was quiet and he presumed they were all still sleeping off the binge.

Then he heard a rumble up front. Suddenly there was heavy, frantic runing down the hall toward him. And Bea burst in on him in her nightgown, her eyes wide with fright. Gulping first, her fingers splayed in the air, she gasped: "You gotta get outa here!—*quick!* Kalandyk's found out! He just called . . . somebody's tipped him off! He knows your name and that you killed that white man and then come here! He's on his way over here! *Right now!* You gotta get outa here fast! He'll kill us both— Jesus God! But if you're gone when he gets here, I can deny I knowed who you was! Otherwise he'd make you talk before he . . . he . . . Lord, get goin'!—get your hat and coat and get outa here! If he ever finds out I brought you here, and all along knowin' who you was, he'll kill me before he does you! *Get goin'!*—and the police could be here any minute too . . . whoever tipped Bertie probably tipped them too! Oh, Lord!—*hurry up!*"

At first he seemed to have suffered a siezure. Then suddenly quivering, he jumped up and put out both hands, palms to the front, as if to push her and the news back out the door. "I can't!" he spluttered. "... I can't! I can't go *out there!* Oh, God, Bea! ... *No!* ... I ..."

"The hell you can't!" she thundered. "That's where you're goin'!" She rushed to the closet, got his coat and hat, and thrust them in his hands. He only stood like a statue. "Did you hear what I said!" she railed. *"Bertie's* on his way here! It's your only chance now, Willie! This is the worst place on God's earth you could be right now—he'll kill you! ... after makin' you talk, he'll kill you without battin' an eye! ... just to get you outa the way before the police get here—he can't do nothin' with that flyin' squad! Why d'you think he's rushin' over here? ... he ain't gonna see this place get knocked over if he can help it!—I'm tellin' you! You at least got some chance out'n the street—but, oh Lord, not here!" She was trying to push, then pull, him toward the door—she was barefoot with large corns on her toes.

His hat and coat in his hands, he still stood speechless, paralyzed, gaping at her.

She stamped her big bare foot on the floor now—"I said *git goin'!*" She grabbed him by the arm and, grunting, pulled him to the door. "You're scared to go out there, but I'm savin' your life, that's whut I'm doin'!" A shoulder strap of her silk nightgown had slipped off her shoulder, baring the top half of one huge, low-hanging breast. She pulled the strap up again and, panting, this time gave him a push—out into the hall. *"Go ahead,* now, Willie! —don't just keep standin' there with your mouth open! Get goin'!—before *Bertie* gets here! . . ."

He finally put on the hat and coat and hurried ahead of her up the hall. Then suddenly he wheeled and seized her by the throat. He lunged with her against the wall and tried to wrestle her to the floor. Yet she was able feebly to cry for help—"Mack! . . . oh, Mack! . . . help me! . . . help me, Mack!" But soon he had her on the floor, his knee in her chest, his circled hands closing to cut off her breathing—the nightgown was up around her neck now, showing her great belly, breasts, and pubic hair. Repeatedly her hands tore at his fingers around her throat as she fought him and tried to cry out again.

Now Mack Thomas swung out of his room. He wore pants and shoes but was naked to the waist. He knelt carefully and got a hand under Yeager's chin and, wrenching up and out, tried to break his neck. But Yeager's hands now throttled Bea's throat. Mack got up and began circling him now, waiting for an opening, and when Yeager flipped over to keep his hold, Mack grunted and kicked him in the testicles. *"Augghhh . . . Augghhh!"* Yeager uttered, and his hands fell away as he doubled up on his side groaning. Then Mack, coolly deliberate, grunting again, viciously kicked him in the head. Blood flew up against the hall wallpaper. Mack still circled.

Bea had jerked her gown down, and, now wheezing and gasping, scrambled to her feet. When she could finally speak, she gave out a gutteral cry—*"Don't!* . . . don't, Mack! Don't kill him! Just git him outa here! . . . but don't kill him!—whut would we do with him? Hurry!— I'll tell you about it later! . . . Git him out!"

Yeager lay stunned and bleeding from the jagged gash across his eye. Mack picked him up now—"Open the door up there," he said to Bea, who had retrieved Yeager's hat. They hurried with him up the hall to the front door, and when Bea, turning the nightlock, had unlocked and opened it, Mack swung him back once and threw him down the steps to the top landing, Bea tossing his hat after him.

When both stepped back inside the door again, Bea, breathing convulsively now, managed to lock it before she uttered an almost childlike cry and clutched at her breast. Then reeling back against the door, she gasped once, looked wide-eyed at Mack, and fell heavily—hitting the floor with her left hip and shoulder. She rolled over on her back in a limp spread-eagle and lay still. Quickly, Mack knelt over her. He looked in her face—"Bea . . . Bea! . . . whut's wrong?" No answer. Although her tongue hung out, her eyes were closed. He shook her by the shoulders once. But got no response. When he could see no breathing, he felt for her wrist pulse. But there was nothing. He knew that she was dead, and his sudden understanding of what it meant—to himself and the others—brought panic to his face. He got up and ran back to get Bismarck.

When he returned with Bismarck, they found Iris standing over her mother's body. ". . . Oh, Lord!" whispered Bismarck—". . . we mighta knowed it."

"Whut's wrong with Mama?" Iris, in her little pants and T-shirt, said to them sternly. "She won't say nothin'."

". . . We don't know," Bismarck said. "Stand back, honey." He got down low on his doddering knees, put his ear flat against Bea's breast, and listened. Mack stood over him, breathing heavily. Finally, his face a mask, Bismarck got up. "Let's git her to her room," he said to Mack. They somehow got their four hands under Bea's heavy body and lugged her back to her room, Iris closely following. Cleo, who had put her head out in the hall, saw them coming with Bea and followed them into her room. They put Bea on the bed on her back and Bismarck covered her to the neck with a sheet.

"Mama's high," Iris said now.

Bismarck and Cleo at this exchanged knowing looks. Finally Cleo went over to Bea and with her thumb pushed Bea's right eyelid open. After a moment she pushed it closed again and turned to Iris. "Your mama's dead," she said.

Iris studied her. Then looked around at the others. "Let her git some sleep, then," she frowned. "When she's like this she gotta sleep it off."

Bismarck looked at Mack and Cleo and, sadly shaking his head, said to them, "The little one don't know that word—'d-e-a-d'—yet, and whut it all means. She thinks Bea's stoned."

Cleo turned to Iris again. "Your mama—"

Just then the doorbell sounded—long and loud.

"Would you git that, Mack?" Bismarck said.

Mack went out and soon admitted apoplectic Kalandyk at the front door. This time Kalandyk had a squat henchman with him.

"Where's Bea!" he demanded, stepping in, his coat wet from the rain. His henchman, following, kept his hand in his coat pocket.

Mack was equally blunt. "I hate to tell'ya, Bertie—Bea just dropped dead of a heart attack."

Kalandyk turned white. ". . . You can't mean it," he finally said. He stood gaping at Mack.

"About ten minutes ago," Mack said. "We just carried her in her room there."

Kalandyk's eyes then narrowed. "Where's that Willie, then?—I wanta see *him.*"

"He's gone. I throwed him out. He jumped on Bea— that's why afterwards she got the heart attack—and I damned near lynched him . . . and throwed him out."

"Good—good, Mack. . . . Did Bea tell'ya anything about him?"

"No. But said she would."

Kalandyk took a deep breath at this, and then, tailed by his man, hurried down the hall toward Bea's room.

He found Mavis and old Jessie now standing over Bea along with the others. Everyone was quiet, self-possessed —including Iris, to whom Cleo, as best she could, had just explained the alien phenomenon of death. Iris seemed, at least for the moment, to accept it, and stood looking on in bewildered, troubled silence.

Kalandyk approached the bier, knelt briefly, and crossed himself. Then he stood looking intently into Bea's reposeful face. "She was a great human bein'," he said to them all, but keeping his eyes on Bea's face. "She was my friend, too. She died tryin' to protect this house and everything in it, and I salute her. She was a strong, awful strong, woman, and knew that's the only way you survive in this jungle-world we come into without bein' asked. Yeah, survive— *that's* what she was interested in. She learned how early, too, believe me—damned early. You folks probably didn't really know her too well—her past. But I did. She told me—she told me it all. And it was somethin' to hear— *somethin'*. Let all these damned do-gooders do their damndest, but they'll never reach cases like hers. She had guts, too—bein' a product of the streets. People like her and me, we make our own deals in life—in our own ways, and by our own laws, and so forth. We live by 'em, too—and then we die by 'em. We don't bellyache. We live!—and sometimes it's tough. Bea done this to the end. Now her struggles are over, and we all hope she's got peace at last."

Iris was listening very intently.

"Nobody could run this place but Bea," Kalandyk said. "Or can, or will. So I gotta tell you, this is the last of the house. Without Bea it's nothin'—when the curtain went down on her, it went down on this house. But I wanta thank all of you. You've been good people, and you won't regret it—you'll have all the time you want to look around and decide what you wanta do, and those that want jobs will get 'em. And you can bet Iris will never see a hungry minute or a needy day—that'll be seen to. In short, we'll do it up the way Bea herself would have approved of, for she liked everyone of youse. So in the next few days you men take charge. . . . you, Bismarck, and Mack . . ." Kalandyk looked around—". . . Where's Donald?"

"He went out," Jessie said. "But he'll be back 'fore long. So did Darlene. I don't know *where* Willie is."

"Okay," Kalandyk said. "Bismarck and Mack, you'll have to get a doctor in here—to pronounce Bea dead and make it official. Then call the undertaker as soon as you can and have him come and get Bea. Tell him not to spare nothing, either—Bea was not cheap and she won't be put away cheap. I'll be back in the morning and we'll all have a meeting to see what's what with everybody. And don't worry—everything's goin' to come out okay for youse." He stopped and meditated. ". . . Only we can't bring Bea back—for that we're damn sorry."

Jessie was dabbing her eyes and sniffling.

Soon they heard someone coming in at the front door. It was Donald. Bareheaded, despite the rain, he had on a new spring topcoat, plaid scarf, and gloves, and was whistling softly as he came down the hall. When he saw all the people in Bea's room, and then Kalandyk, he slowed, then stopped short, staring. At last he saw Bea on the bed, and his mouth fell open. His eyes excited, flighty, he ran in the room—*"What's wrong!"* he cried, incipient terror in his voice. He ran to the bed, but then wheeled around to them all—"Bea's sick!" he said, in nearly a whisper. "Bea's sick . . . *ain't* she!"

Cleo came up beside him then—"She's dead, Donald."

He slowly turned and looked at Cleo for a moment, almost as if he were trying to recall something, then whirled around to Bea again. *"Bea-e-e-e-e!"* he screamed, and fell across her body shrieking and sobbing. *"Bea-e-e-e!* Oh, Bea, don't leave me! . . . what will I *do* without you! . . . you're the only friend I've got, have *ever* had, in all the world. The *only* one! Always, always, everybody else has hated me—loathed me! But not you, Bea, baby—you took me in! . . . you told me I was as good as anybody else! You were my friend—my sweet friend!—now you've gone and left me alone with no friends! What will happen to me now!" He collapsed in wild, frantic sobbing.

Jessie was crying now—"Whut will happen to *all* of us?" she said in a trembling voice. "Jesus, have mercy!"

At last Iris, looking around at the others, crinkled up her face in distress, but cried only briefly. She was too awed, overpowered, by these important events engulfing her.

Donald went on sobbing over Bea until finally Mavis, her eyelashes wet, came and pulled him away. They stood in a corner as Donald continued weeping uncontrollably. *"Think* of me," he said to her. "I don't have a friend in the world now! . . . not one."

Kalandyk stood silent in the middle of the room, his head on his chest.

Soon old Jessie said to them all: "Less hold hands, my friends, and sing somethin'—ah, like they would do in the olden days—somethin' upliftin', comfortin', like Bea's favorite hymn. You-all know whut it was, all right—you heard her sing it many a time. She didn't b'long to no church or anythang but she loved this song, right on. So less sing it, all the verses—it's 'Precious Lord,' of course —and then go on to our rooms; the heart can stand only so much. All right, join hands, now, and I'll lead it and you-all come in strong—in sweet memory of Bea, bless her heart." Taking Cleo's hand, Jessie began singing in her high, ancient, quavering voice. Kalandyk and his man stood respectfully apart and were silent, while the others joined hands around the bed—Mavis singing alto; sorrowing Donald, tenor; Mack, bass; old Jessie, leading— and all sang in a melodious, emotional, exhorting long meter the first of the numerous stanzas of the old hymn:

"Precious Lord, take my hand,
Lead me on, help me stand;
I am tired, I am weak, I am worn;
Through the storm, through the night,
Lead me on to the light;
Take my hand, Precious Lord,
Lead me on. . . ."

Finally, after singing the many stanzas of the hymn, tears coursing down their cheeks, they let go their neighbors' hands and stopped; but for a moment stared in space. Kalandyk and his man now went out unobtrusively, and the others, silent, subdued, troubled, filed out to their rooms.

Chapter 13

AFTER Mack Thomas had thrown Yeager bodily down the steps, Yeager, though only half conscious from the brutal encounter, remembered hearing the door slammed and the nightlock locked again, and he lay there dazed on the stairs' top landing for at least two minutes. At last he stirred weakly—then tried to get up, but could not. But when his mind sufficiently cleared, he remembered. He jumped up, wheeled and got his hat, and stumbled pell-mell down the remaining two and a half flights of stairs into the vestibule. He carefully peered out for a moment, and got out his handkerchief and as best he could mopped the blood off his face. Then, although his legs were slack and wobbly, he left the vestibule and started trotting sideways up the street—but soon he was loping along in a half-crouch because of his throbbing groin. There was a steady drizzle coming down, and he kept close to the buildings, yet not knowing where he would go— again he was the man in flight to nowhere.

He decided to cross the street and go one block over to Beecher Avenue, where the buses ran. Suddenly, over on the opposite curb, he saw her. She was running toward him in the drizzle—Darlene!

"Willie! Willie!" she said—"Come back the other way, over on 23rd Street! Don't go over there—there's too many squad cars hangin' around on Beecher. Come on, let's go over to 23rd and get a taxi. . . . Good Lord—what happened to your face! Come on—this way!"

He turned and pliantly followed her. "Why did you do it?" he said.

She ignored the question. "What happened?" she asked again—"I knew you had to come out pretty soon." They were on the sidewalk now, headed back in the opposite direction, toward 23rd Street—an area of poor businesses and dinky taverns.

". . . Where *is* there a cab!" he said. Fearful, impatient, he rushed ahead dabbing at his eye with the bloody handkerchief.

"Wait! . . . slow down!" she whispered. "You're walkin' too fast—you'll attract attention. Who beat you up?—Mack?"

He was dour and for a moment did not answer her. "Yes," he finally said—"It was your fault. Why did you do it?"

She was silent.

When they reached 23rd Street, they went a block north —to the taxi stand. But there were no taxis. Yeager trembling from fright now, his face bloody, was frantic at having to wait. He pulled his hat far down over his eyes and stood sullen, bitter. She looked at him and sighed, but otherwise her face was expressionless. Now she raised her hand to her head and felt her natural. It and her coat were sodden from the rain.

He suddenly turned to her, his face distressed—"Where are we *going!*"

"To the bus station. We're leavin' town."

"Leaving town! . . . where to?"

"Keep your shirt on, will'ya? You'll find out."

Now he was looking around fearfully in all directions —"We just can't stand here!" Soon he started to leave.

"Oh, Willie! . . ." she said sorrowfully, but was about to follow him—when a taxi arrived at the stand. He rushed back over and clambered in ahead of her. When she finally got in, she gave the driver directions: "We wanta go across the river bridge, over to Maple Street—the 1400 block."

At the words "river bridge" Yeager stiffened—then shuddered. The prospect of looking down from that bridge again into those dark, swirling waters, the grisly flashback, the horror, the grief, filled him with a dread he felt he could not endure. As the taxi pulled off, he began writhing. "That's not the way to the bus station! . . ." he said to her.

"Shhhh!"—she leaned against him and whispered— "We're goin' to the *westside* station. There ain't as many people use it as the one downtown. Willie . . . we're goin' to Chicago."

He turned to her—astonished. He shook his head—
"You know we'll never make it." Taking a deep breath,
he gazed out at the shabby buildings and passing traffic.
They rode for the next ten minutes in silence.

When at last the taxi was approaching the river bridge,
his feeling of revulsion, of sickened panic, almost over-
whelmed him, and he closed his eyes. At once, it seemed,
Florrie's face swam into his mind's blind vision. In awe
he saw her pleasant, sad features—the yellow complexion,
the stubborn, brownish hair, the quizzical eyes, the flat, cute
nose. She seemed calm, unperturbed, as if they were sitting
at home in their living room, and she had looked past him
at some random object as she told him tomorrow she'd
like some fresh strawberries. He now wrung his hands and
gave a tormented sigh. When the cabbie finally drove onto
the bridge, Darlene, remembering, glanced fearfully at
him. His eyes were still tightly, painfully, shut. Suddenly
she reached over and took his hand. She held it until they
had crossed the bridge and gone almost a block on the
other side. When finally she let it go, he opened his eyes
and stared at her as if for a moment he did not know
where he was. Then he peered out at the big Texaco sign
on his right and the new grade school beyond it. Suddenly, frowning, he whispered to her—"Don't let him
take us all the way to the station!"

"I won't," she said.

The taxi had turned into the 800 block on Maple Street now and was heading north toward the 1400's. When shortly afterwards it entered the 1200 block, Darlene stopped the driver, paid the fare, and they got out. Silent, preoccupied, riven with fear, they walked the remaining two blocks to the bus station.

The little station was situated in the middle of a block of neater store fronts and small businesses. Inside, though clean and comfortable—with five seated travelers waiting —it afforded only two long benches for its patrons, plus a tiny ticket window. The ticket agent, who saw them enter, was stout and red-faced, with a bulbous nose. When Yeager saw him looking at his bloody, battered eye, he went at once into the men's room to wash his face. But Darlene walked casually up to the little ticket window and opened her purse.

"Two tickets to Chicago," she said quietly. "When's the next bus?"

The ticket agent reached up in his rack for the pair of tickets. "Next one's at 5:40," he said. She looked at her wristwatch. It was 3:10.

When she had paid the man and put the tickets in her purse, she went over and sat down on the second bench and at the end nearest the door. At last she looked down at her feet. Her shoes and stocking were soaked.

When Yeager returned, he looked fresher, but had clumsily splashed water on his shirt and coat. He sat down beside her and stared at the floor.

"Why did you do it?" he asked once more, but in a kind of singsong voice now, his gaze far, far out the window.

". . . I don't know," she said.

"We can't get away with it. You know that, don't you?"

"Yes . . . not for long anyway."

"You said I'd have to pay. The time's almost come."

"Don't hurry it up, Willie."

"Why did you tip them off?"

She was silent.

"Darlene, why did you do it?"

She sighed. "Maybe I was thinkin' about myself, I don't know. It wasn't you so much."

"Don't lie."

"I'm not lyin'."

"I'm not worth it. Of course, you know that, though."

"Well . . . it was a whole lota things, maybe. Oh, it's too complicated." She looked down at her wet feet, then pulled them back to hide them. "And I wanted to get away from Bea—from that house—after you talked to me. I wonder who she'll get to take our place."

"She'll find somebody, don't worry. Darlene, that place will go on forever."

"We won't know about it, though. We won't be there."

"It would have been better for us to stay," he said.

"Oh, Willie! . . . that's awful! You can see—you ain't changed none."

"We'll do well even to get *to* Chicago."

"Yes . . . I know it."

"I ought to go give myself up. What's the use stringing it out for just a few more days? Even if we do get there, we'll be lucky to have a week together."

She seemed surprised, dismayed. "Oh, why, a week together's a long time," she said. "We ain't known each other for a week yet."

The slow, oppressive rain continued to fall and for a moment they were afraid to look at each other.